FALL *of the* DAWNSTAR

FALL *of the* DAWNSTAR

The Beginning of the Beginning

T. Joel Fairley

This is a work of fiction. All of the characters, names, incidents, organizations, and dialogue in this novel are either the products of the author's imagination or are used fictitiously.

Archway Publishing books may be ordered through booksellers or by contacting:

Archway Publishing
1663 Liberty Drive
Bloomington, IN 47403
www.archwaypublishing.com
844-669-3957

Because of the dynamic nature of the Internet, any web addresses or links contained in this book may have changed since publication and may no longer be valid. The views expressed in this work are solely those of the author and do not necessarily reflect the views of the publisher, and the publisher hereby disclaims any responsibility for them.

ISBN: 978-1-6657-5182-7 (sc)
ISBN: 978-1-6657-5181-0 (hc)
ISBN: 978-1-6657-5259-6 (e)

Library of Congress Control Number: 2023921419

Print information available on the last page.

Archway Publishing rev. date: 01/22/2024

In loving memory of my dear friend Rev. Martin Rolfs-Massaglia and my mom, Carol Fairley, and my Pop, Lowell Fairley, some of the brightest lights that ever did shine.

CONTENTS

PART 1

PART 2

PART 1

THE FIRST

"Open your eyes."

These were the first words he heard. He could not remember anything else beyond those words. They were spoken from somewhere beyond him, outside himself, but close enough to assure he was not alone. The voice that transported the gentle command was warm and full of what he would come to know as affection. He smiled at the knowledge that he even knew how to do what the voice was asking. He opened his eyes.

In the eyes of the One who looked at him, he saw something else. As he lifted his hand to point and as his lips began to form the question "Who?" he saw the "something else" lift its hand and saw its lips form the shape of a small circle as if to say, "Who?" In the next moment, he came to realize he was seeing himself reflected in the eyes of the One.

He was not as bright as the One before him, but he could see that he was a creature of light and great beauty. Though there was nothing to compare himself to, other than the One, he was statuesque. His legs and arms were long and muscular. The fingers on his hands moved with a graceful strength. His body shimmered with a golden hue as the light moved and danced over it, from his feet to the hair on his head.

Starting with his hands, he began to move. He stretched his arms out over his head and down to his waist. He raised his leg and took a step with confidence. The step became a dozen and then a skip, a run, and a leap, which all evolved into a glorious dance. He was dancing because he could, because he was alive and in the presence of the One. With a great leap into the air, he began to spin faster and faster until he was lost in a twirling bright blur. His arms and hands were flung outward, and ribbons of golden light streamed from his fingertips. The light spiraled above and below him, and the One clapped in delight as He watched the movements of His new creation.

The feeling of joy he'd experienced when he first opened his eyes grew exponentially as he danced in the air. What he was feeling in that moment were new sensations to him, which he welcomed with a wide and open heart. They seemed to be centered on a growing appreciation and affection for the One. As the joy of the One became more visible and vocal through His applause and laughter, so did his own joy as he swirled and rose into the air.

Wherever he had been before, if he'd been anywhere, there was no place he would rather be than in the presence of the One. This was his life, and a glorious life it was.

He completed his dance, landed gracefully on his feet, and fell back into the One, laughing. He laughed a long time until it ended in a deep satisfying sigh of contentment. He was still for quite a while as he rested in the arms of the One. A warm, gentle baritone voice brought him out of his silent revelry.

"Do you know who I am?"

"I do." He smiled. "You are the One who told me to open my eyes."

"Yes."

"You gave me life."

"Yes."

"You let me dance."

"Yes."

He was quiet for a moment. Then he declared, "You are the One."

With a quiet tone of authority, He said, "I am. I am the One. I am."

There were no other sounds until the new creation asked in a childlike manner, "Who am I?"

"You are the first," said the One. "The first of a great host."

He smiled at the answer and sank deeper into the presence of the One. "What am I called?" he asked.

"You are called Lucifer," declared the One. "The Light Bringer. You are the Dawn Star."

The answer made the newly christened Dawn Star smile as he closed his eyes, settled peacefully in the arms of the One, and rested.

THE ONE

The Dawn Star opened his eyes for the second time. Upon seeing the One's face, all the sensations he'd felt before returned in a flood of delight, which seemed to mirror that of the One's own delight.

As he took in the sight of the One, he observed similarities between himself and the One, as well as vast differences. While the Dawn Star seemed to be a singular personality, he was aware of three within the One. They were not three parts of the One; they were all the One, complete and whole in themselves as individual personalities yet complete and whole as the One—the Father, the Son, and the Holy Spirit, as he eventually would come to know them.

The One was completely engulfed and surrounded by light. At the center of what could only be described as glory, the character and features of the One were distinctly defined by light. Within the One, the Dawn Star could see a brighter light, which was the heart of the One. Around the One's heart, a legion of much smaller lights orbited as individual constellations. Their tiny dance made the Dawn Star smile curiously.

The glory stretched above and beyond the One. It radiated and danced around Him. The glory of the One engulfed and pulsated on the Dawn Star in comforting waves of love and joy. The glory seemed to originate from the very heart of the One. It was the source of the One's great love.

His love was something that he could feel …

Something that he could see …

Something that the Dawn Star could hear in a song that seemed to have no end.

He breathed it in as the priceless fragrance it was. He feasted on it as a banquet. He was completely nurtured and satisfied by the love that came from the very heart of the One.

When he was able find his breath again, the Dawn Star said in a deep sigh, "Oh, Lord, You are good." Then, timidly, he asked, "May I call You Lord?"

"Yes, you may. I like that," the One replied gently.

To the Dawn Star, the One seemed to be immense and without limits but at the same time close and personal. This characteristic made the Dawn Star's Lord a wonder to him. He was in childlike wonder of the One. He reached out to touch the glory as if to take it into himself. He observed the face of the One become that of the Father, then the Son, and then the Holy Spirit. He desired to know better each of them as he gazed at the One. The tiny constellations around the heart of the One continued to dance in time to the song of God's glory.

The Dawn Star pointed to the dancing points of light and asked, "What are those?"

"They are that which is yet to come. They are the essence of all that will soon be made by My hand."

"Was I made by Your hand?" the Dawn Star asked.

"You were," answered the One.

He wondered for a moment and then asked, "Whose hand made You?"

The One's gentle voice grew stronger. "I have always been as I am. I am uncreated. There was no one before Me, and no one will come after Me. I am the Lord, your God, and there is none other besides Me."

The hand of the One reached forward to caress the face of the Dawn Star. "Do you understand?" He asked.

The Dawn Star leaned his face into the loving hand of the One who made him and nodded. "I do," he said. "You are the Lord, my God."

"I am," said the One.

At that moment, the Dawn Star felt the immensity of the One. He sensed that God had gone beyond the boundaries of his young understanding to a comprehension that was completely unique and isolated to the mysteries of the One's thoughts.

As he continued to feel the One's intense love, a feeling of mystery and wonder overwhelmed the Dawn Star. Before, upon discovering the One for the first time, he'd danced, leaped, and twirled and had then sunk into the presence of God to get closer and deeper, as if to possess more of Him. Now he felt the awesome, mighty, mysterious power that was God, and he kept his distance and did the only thing he knew in his heart to do. The Dawn Star bowed down to worship the One.

"You are the Lord God, my maker," proclaimed the Dawn Star. "There is none like You."

And the One smiled, poured out love on him, and said, "It is good."

3

THE CITY OF GOD

"I want to show you our home," said the One to the Dawn Star.

"Our home?" the Dawn Star asked.

"Yes, where you and the others will be with Me," He answered.

"The others?"

"Yes, the ones who will come after you. You were the first, but there will be more, many more. They will be a great host, a heavenly host. They will be like you but not like you. Each will be different according to My own design."

"And we will all live here with You?" the Dawn Star asked.

"Yes. We shall all live in the city of God," the Lord declared.

The Dawn Star looked around and became aware that he was standing in the middle of a great room. As he took notice of where he stood, he saw it was immense, with pearl columns that rose and vaulted into a ceiling that seemed to be a vast extension of the glory of God.

"What is this place?" he asked.

"It is My holy temple," the Lord declared. "The place where my presence is best known."

The floor upon which he stood was as a polished jewel, and the walls gleamed like gold. As he took it all in, he saw two tall doors at the end of the hall open out to a vista filled with a swirling mist and golden clouds.

"Come," the One said as he took the Dawn Star by the hand and led him toward the opened doors. "Come and see."

When they passed through the doors, they stood on the threshold of the temple. The golden clouds extended to a far horizon wherever he turned his head. God's temple seemed to float on this gilded, undulating sea like a vessel of light, anchored only by a staircase that descended into the swirling golden mist.

In the clouds the Dawn Star could see vague outlines of other structures that appeared through the haze and then quickly disappeared like a promising mirage.

Once in a while, the waves of clouds parted long enough to reveal towering spires reaching out to the light above them, but barely long enough for the Dawn Star to get a detailed glimpse before the clouds washed over them again as if they only existed in a dream.

"I see something, but I am not quite sure," the Dawn Star said.

"You are getting glimpses of what my city will be," the One replied. "For now, it is hidden until its full purpose becomes necessary."

The Dawn Star enjoyed the mysterious dance of the clouds as bits and pieces of God's city appeared and then quickly disappeared. A smile came to his face each time a shape or spire winked into view like the promise of an amazing gift yet to be given.

"What could they be?" he wondered aloud. "What will be their purpose?" He thought of the others the One had spoken of, those who would be like him but different. "Is this where they will all live?"

The Dawn Star turned around and looked up at the holy temple with its gleaming walls and majestic columns that rose high above him to support the roof, which rested on the temple like a crown of glory. Rays of light beamed out from the top in straight and angular lines stretching out to infinity.

"I want to live here," he said as he looked into face of God. "I want to live here with you."

The Lord smiled warmly at the Dawn Star. "You are with me."

After a moment, he resumed taking in the heavenly vista that surrounded the temple. When he glanced toward the golden staircase, a shadow appeared from below it and solidified into a shape that did not disappear like the others before it.

"What is down there?" the Dawn Star asked.

God smiled and said, "It is something I think you will love. Would you like to see?"

A joyous fountain of emotions surged up with in him as he exclaimed, "Oh yes!"

"Then take my hand," the Lord said.

They stepped together down from the temple's threshold and descended the staircase to what waited below. The Dawn Star wasn't sure if they were walking or floating down the stairs. Because his senses were so occupied with other matters, he barely noticed the particulars of the descent. When he was with the One, he barely noticed his own actions. The wonder of God and His works filled him up so completely that it nearly blocked out everything else around him.

So filled with emotion in the presence of the Lord, the Dawn Star scarcely realized that the mist cleared from the staircase with each step they took in their descent toward what waited for them below. When their journey was complete, the gold mist had completely dispersed and the Dawn Star found himself standing in front a pair of great jade doors that belonged to what could only be described as a palace. The structure gleamed in gold as it reflected the light of God's temple above it at the top of the great staircase.

The Dawn Star reached out to touch the green doors, which were ornately engraved with symbols and words that he did not yet comprehend. As he traced his finger along the designs, he noticed a glow from inside the palace through the semi-translucent doors.

"What is this place?" the Dawn Star asked.

"It is the palace of all things," the Lord answered.

"All things?"

"All the wisdom and knowledge for that which is to come is here."

The Dawn Star took in the One's answer in rapt silence. After a moment, in a quiet, timid, but excited voice, he asked, "May I see?"

The Lord laughed out his answer in a soothing baritone. "Yes! I would love to show you."

As He pushed the doors open, the One turned to the Dawn Star and said, "Please come inside. I have a gift for you."

IN THE PALACE OF ALL THINGS

The Dawn Star and the One stood in a large circular room in the center of a twelve-pointed star designed into the floor. The four longest points of the star jutted ninety degrees out from the center, each pointing to four large sets of doors, including the one through which they had just walked. When they entered the room from the outside, they walked over the longest point of the star's design. It was nearly twice the length as the other three longest points.

The Dawn Star studied the design on the floor and wondered at its similarity to something else. He looked at the One, who stood next to him. He looked into the center of the One and smiled when he realized that the star on the floor was designed after the very heart of God. He saw it there, shining forth from the One, with the same four points of the heart star extending farther than the other eight points. Two jutted straight out from the sides, and two extended to the top and bottom, with the bottom point extending twice as long as the other three.

The Dawn Star pointed to the design on the floor and then to the center of the One.

"This is Your heart, isn't it?"

The One smiled and said, "Yes, it is." As he spoke, the constellations orbiting the heart of God twinkled a little bit brighter.

"This is the palace of all things you say?"

"Yes," said the One.

"So," said the Dawn Star, "all things come from the Heart of God?" As he said this, one of the constellations crisscrossed and danced around God's heart.

The Dawn Star felt nothing but love emanating from the One's heart, and he mused to himself that all things therefore must come from the love of God. The One smiled at the Dawn Star as if to affirm his thoughts.

He looked around the rest of the room and saw that the ceiling stretched out high above him. The Dawn Star could also see that there were other levels with doors spiraling up and around the room toward the ceiling.

"What is up there?" he asked.

"Let's find out," said the One as he rose up, surrounded by His glory.

The Dawn Star watched the One rise above him toward the ceiling. With all his heart, he wished to follow the One as He ascended. As if his wishes were words spoken, the One answered the Dawn Star's desire by extending a hand down toward him and releasing a ball of light like a gleaming star that descended and burst all over him. Lucifer bowed his head and closed his eyes as the brightness of God's glory swiftly engulfed him.

When the light subsided, he felt a slight heaviness at his back and between his shoulders. It was not an unpleasant sensation by any means. He looked over his shoulders, first to his left and then to his right, and saw two great wings twice the length of his arms extending from his shoulder blades on each side. They undulated back and forth in anticipation of what would come next. The Dawn Star gasped in astonishment and delight as he took in this new gift from God.

When he could no longer contain the joy welling up within him, he burst up from the floor with a flap of his wings and ascended to be alongside the One. The Dawn Star would have liked to fly higher, but to do so would have taken him farther away from the Lord, and he did not want that. As great a sensation as it was to fly, it did not match the overwhelming experience of being close to the One.

The One ascended through the palace of all things with the Dawn Star close by his side. As they passed many levels, Lucifer could see that along with the doors that spiraled around the great hall, there were corridors and hallways with even more doors that led to places that were a mystery to him.

"What are those?" the Dawn Star asked as he spun around as if trying to point at every hallway and door he saw.

The One smiled and said, "Those are the Doors of Different Possibilities."

"There are so many," declared the Dawn Star.

"Because there are many possibilities," said the Lord.

"When will the doors be opened?" he asked.

The One paused a moment and, in a slightly grave tone, answered, "When another possibility is needed."

"Do you know what's behind each door?"

"I do," said the One. "All that is here within the palace of all things has been the work of my hands."

In all innocence, the Dawn Star asked, "When will a possibility be needed?"

The One looked at the Dawn Star in loving silence and then said, "When certain choices are made." Before the Dawn Star could ask the question forming on his lips, the One said, "Come. I have more to show you."

They glided to just below the ceiling of the great hall, and the Dawn Star saw the same pattern that he called "the heart of God" designed into the ceiling. The same fourth point extended farther than the others.

The Dawn Star smiled to himself as he thought, *If I turn myself upside down and stand on the ceiling, I could be at the beginning again.*

He felt the One squeeze his hand as He said, "Look."

At the top of the great hall with the ceiling, windows surrounded them instead of doors and corridors. The One was pointing at one of these windows to something He wanted the Dawn Star to see. Lucifer turned and looked. He saw the great staircase they had descended to reach the palace of all things. At the top of the staircase, high above them, was the glowing, vibrant presence of the temple of God.

The Dawn Star's breath caught in his throat as he looked upon its majestic splendor. He thought it was the most beautiful thing he had ever seen, with the One's beauty being the only exception. The Dawn Star turned to the One and embraced Him in all His glory, for he was filled with so much awe, wonder, and love that there was nothing else he could say or do. And at the very top of the palace of all things, in the shadow of His holy temple, the One hugged him back.

A DOOR IS OPENED

When the Dawn Star moved away from the One, he discovered that they were back down on the floor. He had no knowledge of how or when they arrived; he only knew that he was standing now in the middle of the great hall, surrounded by four sets of doors with the One by his side.

The Dawn Star walked around the One to study the doors pensively. The other three sets of doors were about three quarters the size of the great jade doors through which they had originally walked. Each set of doors was a different color—golden yellow, violet, and green—and looked as if it were each made from a precious stone.

"Shall we see what's inside?" the One asked as He swept his hand across, indicating the three sets of doors.

"Yes!" the Dawn Star burst out with an excitement he could barely contain.

With that, the topaz doors on the left of the hall began to open. The Dawn Star and the One walked toward them as they swung wide to reveal the secret behind them. They walked into the room now open before them. It was a long great hall, almost five stories tall. Along the walls, the Dawn Star noticed long gleaming objects of varying lengths and thicknesses, each with a sharp point on one end and what seemed to be a handle on the opposite end.

"What is this room?" the Dawn Star asked.

"This is the room of readiness," the One replied. "When certain possibilities are made known, this room will be needed."

The Dawn Star looked at one of the gleaming objects on the walls. "And this?"

"It is called a sword," said the One.

"What is it for?"

The One was silent for a moment. "For a purpose known only to me for now."

Though another question was forming in his mind, the Dawn Star kept it in its place as he looked into the direct gaze of the One.

As they walked through the hall, the Dawn Star noticed the individual beauty of each sword. Some were curved, some were straight, and some had blades thicker than others. There were some that were very simple in their construction and others that were much more elaborate with beautiful designs etched into the blades.

When the Dawn Star looked at the swords, he felt excitement as well as caution. There was a quiet solemnity surrounding the objects in the hall, as if they were waiting for their awesome, terrible, holy, and mysterious purpose to be revealed.

The One plucked one of the swords off the wall and handed it to the Dawn Star. Lucifer took it gently in his hand. His eyes were wide, as he did not know what to expect from holding it. It was a long, slightly curved blade that was simple in its structure. Holding it out away from him, he immediately felt as if it were an extension of his own hand. There was a slight thrill in his arms as he gingerly moved it up and down and from side to side as he tested its weight. After a little while, he swung it from left to right, making a great *swoosh* in the air, and smiled at the sound. He swooshed it again, delighted by the sound and the gleam reflecting off the blade.

Suddenly, he spread the new gift of his wings and lifted off the floor with the sword held straight above him. At a certain level, he extended his sword clear out from his side and spun around in the air, laughing with delight. As he spun, the sword sang out a low whir as it cut through the air faster and faster. The sound of the sword grew louder as streams of light swirled around the Dawn Star. The One smiled as He watched him participate in what could only be described as playing.

After the game was over, the Dawn Star descended to the floor and handed the sword back to the One. "Thank you," he said.

"Was that fun?" the One asked as he placed the sword back on the wall.

The Dawn Star nodded quickly and responded with a simple, "Uh-huh."

As they continued their exploration of the room of readiness, the Dawn Star, with the One as his guide, discovered other instruments that he learned were called shields, breastplates, and helmets hanging on the walls, along with more swords in racks on the floor. The great room was filled with these things, the ultimate purpose of which was known only to God. The Dawn Star wondered what they were for. Surely their use went beyond the game he played earlier with the sword. He was content to let his questions go unanswered, for he found himself trusting in the One's mysterious purpose and the wisdom that surrounded it.

At the far end of the room, the Dawn Star was taken aback by the presence of a large clear box in middle of the floor. Suspended in the center of the case was a large sword with a blade that seemed to be made of a bluish fire. Lucifer was mesmerized by the flaming sword. Again, questions about its purpose flooded him, but he kept them unspoken.

As if the One heard his silent inquiries, He said, "I will say its purpose is for good when it is time to remove it from this place. It was made for a holy and good purpose, as were all the weapons in this room."

Lucifer had no meaning for the word *weapon* beyond what he had used the sword for in his game. In his innocence, the Dawn Star discerned that the holy and good purpose God was speaking of could be something fun, like twirling in the air with a gleaming sword in his hand and listening to the sound it made as it swooshed through the air.

Knowing what he was thinking, the One looked lovingly into his golden eyes and said, "My precious Dawn Star, I love you and desire for you to be with me always. Please know that my ways are good and holy."

Lucifer looked at the flaming sword. Its flame bathed his face in a bluish hue. "I know you love me, and I am pleased to be here at your side." He paused and looked into the One's face. "And I know you are good."

As the Lord took the Dawn Star by the hand to continue their journey through the hall, Lucifer said, "I wonder what kind of sound that sword makes when it swooshes through the air."

At that statement, the One put his head back and broke forth in so joyous a laugh that all the swords vibrated on the walls. As he continued to laugh, a force of light and stars erupted out from him and burst into a cascade of light and color against the ceiling.

The Dawn Star added his own laughter to God's when he realized his own joke. He wondered why so awesome a weapon would even have a swoosh at all. The fireworks of their amusement continued as they completed their journey through the room of readiness.

ANOTHER DOOR OPENS

When they walked out of the room of readiness hand in hand, the One led the Dawn Star through the great hall to the emerald doors directly across from where they had just come. As they drew nearer, the doors began to swing open. Compared to the room of readiness, which was quiet and still as it waited for its mysterious purpose to be revealed, the room that was now opened wide before them seemed alive with pictures, sound, and energy.

The Dawn Star couldn't help but be excited as he beheld what was before him. The glory of the One next to him seemed to grow brighter as they entered the room. The images and sounds became louder and brighter as well, as if they were reflections of the glory of God, which in a way they were or would be.

The room itself was quite emense with a ceiling that vaulted high above the Dawn Star's head. Its vastness was a paradox in that the space, which seemed to have no boundaries, was contained in its entirety within the confines of the palace of all things.

There were many levels and balconies throughout the room, all of which were furnished with shelves, cabinets, and cases. In these, as the Dawn Star would come to learn, were a vast variety of books, scrolls, tablets, charts, and papers. There were even books stacked on the floor like great columns against the walls of the room. The images and sounds that moved about the room in a joyous dance seemed to be emanating from these books, scrolls, papers, and charts.

The Dawn Star's eyes grew wide with the wonder of it all.

"What is this place?" he asked in one excited breath.

The One paused and looked around the room in a full circle. "This is my Logos, the Room of My Word," the One said with loving satisfaction.

The Dawn Star cocked his head to one side. "Your word?"

"Everything that has been, everything that is to be, and everything that will be, according to my plan and design, is written here and contained in this room down to the last detail."

The Dawn Star pointed at one of the many pictures dancing around the room. "What are they?"

"These are the images of my creation, that which is to come."

As one of the images came closer, the Dawn Star tried to capture it, but his hand passed through it, for it had no corporeal form.

The One smiled. "These are only the designs of what will be. My word has yet to be made manifest in my creation. They are only an idea now, but soon ..." God left the rest of the sentence go unsaid as He looked at the swirling and twirling images surrounding Him.

The Dawn Star desired to see more of the treasures contained in the room of God's word. The One responded to his desire as if it were spoken: "Come. Let me show you something," he said, as he led the Dawn Star to a tall cabinet.

When the cabinet doors were open, he saw that it was filled with many rolled-up charts stacked neatly next to the other, each in their own compartment and all in a row. The rows extended to the entire length of the cabinet. Selecting one from the middle of the cabinet, the One unrolled it in the air, and there it stayed as he explained to the Dawn Star what was written on it.

"This is the path that the east wind will take when it blows."

The Dawn Star did not yet know what an east wind was or what the symbols and numbers on the chart could possibly mean, but his heart beat faster with excitement as he gazed upon them.

The Lord produced other charts. "And this is for the north wind, and this one for the south, and this for the west. And these …" He paused as many more charts appeared and were unrolled around them. "These are the plans for the breezes. And this …" he said as he pointed to a chart that hung above them. "This is for that which would be called a zephyr, a gentle breeze."

The Dawn Star smiled at the sound of the word. He liked how it made his mouth feel when he repeated it.

With mounting excitement, the One said, "More, I want to show you more."

With that word, the charts around them immediately returned to their places in the tall cabinet. God took the Dawn Star by the hand and led him on a tour of the wondrous room of God's word.

They passed shelves of books that had titles like *The Depths of the Sea: Volume 25* and a thick one titled *Boundaries, Rules, and Statutes of the Ocean Tides*. The Dawn Star saw other books called *When Swallows Return* and *How Tall a Cedar Grows* and many more about subjects he did not yet understand.

As God and His glory passed, images of the different books' subject matter came forth and joined the other pictures that hovered around the One.

They traveled through the room with all the images of God's

Word following close by until they came to another pair of closed and locked doors. There was a gold seal that served as a lock; it bore the same image of the heart star that was on the floor and ceiling of the great hall. When the One placed his hand on the door's handle, the seal seemed to melt away and the doors opened to receive their guests.

The One and the Dawn Star walked into a large round room with a domed ceiling. The doors closed behind them. The images remained outside, so the room felt quiet, still, and reverent.

Along the walls of the room were more shelves filled with more books and scrolls. Sitting on one of the shelves was a stack of papers sealed with the image of the heart star. On a sealed paper at the top of the stack, the Dawn Star read, "Orders for the Morning." Upon seeing something else, and with the One's unspoken permission, the Dawn Star picked up a book titled, *The Foundations of the Earth.*

"What is the Earth?" the Dawn Star asked.

The Lord said, "Here. I will show you."

He indicated with His hand a large scroll that sat in the middle of a round table in the center of the room. The scroll had a large scarlet ribbon wrapped around it with the words "The heavens and the Earth" written on it.

Lucifer moved close to the One as He touched the words and the ribbon fell easily away. The Dawn Star stood quietly as he watched God slowly open the scroll.

Images of bright spiraling lights against a dark background appeared above them. The Dawn Star moved even closer to the One, not sure of what he was seeing.

The One smiled and said in a quiet, comforting tone, "This will be the universe, and these will be called galaxies."

As the scroll unfurled more, images of galaxies appeared on the dark background.

"Ah, there it is," the One said as one particular pinwheel of light joined the others above them.

The Dawn Star watched as the Lord reached up to touch the new arrival. As He did, the galaxy grew and became larger and took the place of the former images above them.

It was a bright shining mass made up of a multitude of smaller lights that streamed out from its large bright center. The One reached out and held the image of the galaxy in one hand. It slowly spun as He inspected it carefully. The Dawn Star observed the Lord smile when He saw something toward the outer edge of the galaxy.

As before, the One moved His hand and pointed at something that was unperceivable to the Dawn Star until a light began to grow on one of the swirling arms of the galaxy and soon replaced it altogether. With its yellowish hue, it was not as bright as the former, but it still seemed to hold sway over the round objects of various sizes and colors that orbited around it.

When one of the smaller blue objects came into view, the One smiled deeply and said, "This …"

As He touched it, the blue ball became bigger and rested in both palms of God's hands. There were no other images now in the room but the slowly spinning blue orb.

"This is the Earth. This will be the home of the beloved."

The Dawn Star was silent. He had no words. He looked at the image of the Earth and into the face of the One next to him and felt once again the tangible presence of love inside this great round room. He felt something else … holiness, though he did not fully comprehend what that would be.

"Thank you for showing me this," the Dawn Star said.

"You are most welcome," came the gentle reply.

After watching the image of the Earth spinning on its tilted axis for a while, the Dawn Star asked, "What is the beloved?"

The One slowly rolled up the scroll and placed the red ribbon around it once again.

"You will know in time," the One finally replied.

The Dawn Star was curious and excited by this response. After what he just saw, the beloved must be the wonder of all wonders.

They walked around the table as the doors of the round room opened, and they rejoined the energy of images and sounds outside the Room of the heavens and the Earth. The Dawn Star turned and watched the doors close behind them. The golden image of the heart star reappeared to seal the doors once again. They continued their tour, and the Dawn Star took in every sight, sound, and new discovery with wide-eyed wonder and joy.

The beauty of it all was overwhelming to the Dawn Star. He felt as if he could not contain his delight, but he had no words or sounds to express what he was experiencing. The only thing he felt he could do was join the images, sounds, and symbols in their dance of wonder.

With his wings, he rose into the midst of them. Everything now seemed to be moving around the One, as did the Dawn Star. They spiraled around each other even as they circled the Lord, who was at the center of their attention. They rose up and down as everything orbited around the One. As the Dawn Star played among the images of strange creatures and symbols, ribbons of light streamed from behind him like a golden wake.

When he thought he would burst from the joy of it all, the Dawn Star flew into the arms of the One, who gently caught him and then playfully tossed him into the air again. They both laughed, sending another cascade of fireworks into and across the cathedral ceiling and among the images of God's creation. As wondrous as everything contained in this room was, nothing compared to the One. Like in the room of God's word, the Dawn Star didn't have the words or a way to adequately express what he felt about all of it … That would soon change.

THE SONGS IN THE TREE

When the doors of the room of God's word closed behind them and they were in the great hall once again, the Dawn Star leaped into the air in a shower of light and flew around in a state of nervous energy.

The One smiled at him. "What are you doing?"

"I don't know," he replied. "I'm just so excited."

"I can see that," the One said.

"I don't know what to say or do … There is so much inside me that I feel I will burst," the Dawn Star said.

He was about to fly higher, but the One caught him by the foot and gently brought him to the floor, saying, "Be at peace, Dawn Star …" The Lord then sat on the floor of the great hall in the middle of the image of the heart star "… and tell me about what you are feeling."

Accepting the One's invitation, the Dawn Star sat on the floor with Him. After sitting still for a few moments, he said, "I love you." With his arms spread above him, the Dawn Star continued, "I love all of this!"

"As I love you."

"I love your word!" he said as he pointed to the emerald doors. "I love the sound of a swooshing sword." He looked toward the room of readiness. "I love that if I fly to the top of this great hall, I will see your holy temple. I love it … I do love it so."

"I am very glad," the One said with a smile.

The Dawn Star went on. "But how do I tell you this?"

The One chuckled. "I think you just did."

The Dawn Star was quiet for a moment and then said, "Words don't seem to be enough. I want more than just words." He pointed to his heart. "In here, there is much more to say, and I wish I could say it, but I don't know how. I don't know the language of my own heart."

The One took the Dawn Star's golden face into His hands and said, "Oh, my precious Dawn Star, you are greatly loved. I know what is in your heart. Let me give you the language to speak it."

The One stood up and led the Dawn Star to his feet, and they began walking toward the amethyst doorway that had yet to be opened. The Dawn Star and the One were standing in front of the violet double doors when the One opened His mouth and began to sing.

The voice of the One as He sang was low and gentle, and the tune sounded as if He had been singing it for an eternity. The language of the song was unknown to the Dawn Star as well. This was yet another mystery that belonged to the One alone. The music was melodic with a haunting beauty all its own, and Lucifer longed for it to go on forever, but it ended in the same low, gentle manner with which it began. Upon the immediate conclusion of the song, the doors of amethyst slowly swung open.

The Dawn Star asked quietly, "What did you just do? What was that sound you made?"

The One smiled and said, "I was singing. I was singing a song that asked the ancient doors to open and reveal the glories found within."

The glories within began with a soft, warm light that spilled out from the open doorway and into the great hall where they stood. The light was accompanied by sounds of music. There seemed to be no specificity to the tune, but it brought a peaceful warmth to the senses as it gently surrounded them. As they walked into the room, the Dawn Star could see the source from which the light and the music originated. In the center of the room stood what the Dawn Star recognized from the books and images in the room of God's word as a large tree.

The enormous tree of a golden green hue seemed rooted to the floor of the palace of all things. Its branches stretched out above the Dawn Star in a wide canopy. The height of the tree was indiscernible from where they stood under its great boughs. The Dawn Star hoped he would be given the chance to discover how high the tree actually grew. The source of the room's warm light came from orbs that hung on the limbs of the tree like glowing fruit. The music also seemed to be emanating from the globes of light.

The One lifted his hands toward the fruit on the tree and said, "Here grows the language of your heart."

The Dawn Star's eyes grew wide with excitement, though he still did not understand fully the secret of the tree and its golden fruit.

"This is the tree of songs. Upon it grow songs of the heavens and the Earth."

The Dawn Star smiled as he thought of the round room, the great scroll, the sparkling galaxies, and the round blue home of the beloved.

"Here also are songs of the Kingdom of God, songs of mysteries and marvels that have yet to be spoken into being ... songs of great joy and immovable truth." The One paused and looked into the eyes of the Dawn Star. "And songs of my boundless, eternal love." He continued, "Come and see."

He took the Dawn Star by the hand, and together they glided to the first large branch of the tree of songs. The Dawn Star stood on the limb as the One sat beside him and pointed to a globe of light nearest to him.

"Pick that one," the One said.

The Dawn Star reached up and took the light fruit into his hands. It came away easily from the tree, and instinctively the Dawn Star brought it to his face and made to sniff it. When he did so, the fruit completely dissipated as he inhaled the light. The light of the fruit flooded his whole being with warmth. It spread from his feet to the tips of his wings. When the warmth settled at his center, he felt something unlock. What was unleashed immediately went to his head with a rush like a refreshing breeze clearing away the dust that covered a hidden treasure.

The Dawn Star's eyes went wide when he discovered for the first time the language of his heart. He opened his mouth, and what came out was not a spoken language but a song.

The Dawn Star stood on the branch and sang the new song. The sound of his own voice was a delight to his ears. Like him, it was full of light and life, strong and vibrant. It echoed against the walls of the great chamber in which the tree grew. He sang a melody of moderate tempo with notes ranging into several octaves. The Dawn Star hit every note precisely, without even the slightest hesitancy.

As he sang, he could see the holy temple of God in his mind's eye, for that was what the song was about. He sang in flawless poetry of the golden staircase, the columns of pearl, and the glory of God that gave light to the entire city of God. It was a song of praise and worship to the One, who dwelled in the temple. Love and joy poured forth from the Dawn Star with every note and word. It truly was the language of his heart.

When the song was complete, he sang it again and then again and countless more times. The One seemed to be as delighted with the song as the Dawn Star was. He sat on the branch and looked upon him with love. Though the song had ultimately come from the One, as did all things, He listened to the song each time as if it were being heard and sung for the first time.

After the last notes of the temple song echoed through the tree, the Dawn Star sat on the limb next to the One with a satisfied sigh. "So that's what was in my heart?" he asked.

"Yes," said the One.

"I love it," he said with a huge smile. "It was exactly what I wanted to say about your holy temple." After a few moments of sitting quietly next to the One, the Dawn Star sprang to his feet and said, "I want to sing it again!"

The One smiled and indicated other fruit hanging from the tree. "There are other songs waiting for you to give them voice."

The Dawn Star swiveled his head around and smiled broadly as he realized the riches in music that surrounded him. "Oh yes!" he said. Indicating another globe, he looked to the One. "May I?"

"Of course!" said the One. "This tree and every song that grows from it are yours."

"Mine?"

"Yes. They are yours to sing, yours to share, yours to teach to others. This is my gift to you, Dawn Star. This is why you were created, to sing the songs of heaven and Earth, to sing the songs of my glory."

The Dawn Star could hardly take in what he was being told by the One. He lifted himself effortlessly through the branches, his wings barely moving. As he glided upward, he took another piece of fruit and let its warmth embrace him. As before, his heart and mind were opened, but this time he sang a ballad about the wonders of God's word as images of the room of God's word appeared in his head to give inspiration to his song.

Upon completion of the word song, he selected another piece of fruit and sang an aria of the galaxies. He flew through the tree branches, singing song after song. Each piece found its way into the Dawn Star's heart to join the others already there. Each song was like a gift in and of itself, never to be forgotten or discarded by him. His heart seemed to be filled to the brim, but there always seemed to be room for another.

He glided back down to sit beside the One and said, "This tree is really mine?"

The One said, "Yes. Do you accept it?"

The Dawn Star slowly took in all that was around him and said softly, "Yes. I accept it … And thank you." He reached up and picked another globe and sang a simple song of thanksgiving to the One, and the One was glad.

When the Dawn Star was finished, the One said with calm authority, "You will be given a host of others, and you will teach them the songs of the tree. They will be the chorus of heaven, and you shall lead them. Do you accept this as well?"

The Dawn Star pondered the One's request. His thoughts went to the others of whom the One spoke. What would they be like? How many would there be? Who would they be? The One had said they would be like him but still unique and different, and he had no concept of what it meant to lead anyone, let alone a chorus of a great host.

The One's voice broke into his thoughts. "I will give you everything you need to lead the host I give you."

The Dawn Star was quiet for a moment. "It won't be just you and me anymore, will it?"

"No," the One said and smiled. "But you will always be my Dawn Star. I will never leave you."

"I will lead a great chorus?"

The One stood and stretched out his hands. "And the city of God will be filled with their voices. The walls will ring with their songs."

The Dawn Star stood and said in an excited voice, "And You. We will sing about You."

The One looked at him with overwhelming love and said softly, "If it would please you to do so."

"It would please me," the Dawn Star replied. "It would please me very much."

"As it would Me," came the One's soft reply. "Do you accept this responsibility as well?"

The Dawn Star looked up at the tree and the multitude of new songs still left on its branches, waiting to be sung. He closed his eyes as if to see the great heavenly choir singing together the songs of heaven and smiled.

"Yes," he said. "I accept."

THE OTHERS

The Dawn Star and the One walked up the golden staircase toward the Lord's temple, leaving the palace of all things and its wonders behind. As they ascended, the Dawn Star talked to the One about all he had seen and experienced there. He ran in front of the One and stood a few stairs above the Lord to tell him about one of the rooms they had visited, as if the One had not been present as his guide and he was making this report to Him for the first time.

"… and the big blue ball spun 'round and 'round …" he said. "… and that's the home of the beloved … and …" Each new detail of his report ran into the next as if they were all part of the same sentence. " … and I made a sword go *swoosh* …" he said from a few more steps higher.

The One simply smiled affectionately as they continued their slow ascent back up to the Lord's temple.

When they had traveled the distance between the palace of all things and temple, the Dawn Star took a short breath as they stood on the threshold before the great open doors of God's holy temple. As beautiful and wondrous and full of mystery as the palace of all things was, it was a modest beauty compared to the glories of the One's home. Though Lucifer had been created in the temple and had viewed it from the top of the great hall, in returning to it, he felt as if he were seeing it for the first time. The walls shining like gold, the columns of pearl, the jeweled floor—it all seemed fresh and new. As he stood on the threshold of the temple, the Dawn Star was overwhelmed with the compulsion to sing as the Spirit of the One engulfed him in His presence.

The temple song poured forth from his golden throat with greater strength, conviction, and love as he stood before the song's inspiration. The sound of his voice echoed off the walls and columns of the temple and filled the entire space. It seemed as if it would fill completely the length and breadth of the city of God.

He continued to sing as he followed the One into the temple.

He sang as he watched the One ascend to a raised dais suspended above the temple floor.

He sang as the One settled upon the dais as if sitting upon a throne.

He sang as the glory of the One cascaded over the dais like the folds of a robe.

He sang the temple song with his head raised toward the One upon His throne.

He sang as he looked upon the loving, powerful, mysterious three-in-one face of the One, complete in its glory.

He sang as the One looked at him in gracious delight.

He sang because it was natural for him to do so.

He sang to bring glory to God upon His throne, and when his song was done, he knelt before the One because it also was natural for him to do so.

When he rose to his feet again, the One was standing by his side.

In the temple, the glory of God seemed brighter and more tangible as if it were a thing unto itself. The Dawn Star would have liked to take some of the glory into his own hand as if to splash his face with it, but it was not his to take. It was his to only receive should the One so graciously offer it to him.

By the light of God's glory, he could see that there was much more to the temple than what he had noticed before. High above and just before the walls connected to the ceiling—which was more like a covering of God's glory than a solid part of a building's structure—were rows of windows whose purpose seemed to be more about letting light out as opposed to bringing light in.

Etched and painted images adorned the walls of gold. These were not like the images that had swirled and danced around them in the room of God's word. To the Dawn Star they seemed as if they only belonged in the temple of the One and His holy city. They were of beings like himself. There were legions of them in a mural that stretched the length of the enormous walls and surrounded the throne of the One.

"They are the host of heaven," said the One by his side.

Taking in the magnitude of scene, the Dawn Star said, "Such a mighty host."

Putting a glorious arm around the Dawn Star's shoulders, the One said, "They will indeed be that, and you are the first among them." As he said this, the One pointed to an image set high and in the center of one of the walls.

He was indicating a figure of golden hue with long, muscular legs and arms that were stretched out as if in praise of something. The figure's hands were turned up, ready to receive or give away that which was put in them. The figure's golden hair cascaded over its shoulders, and its golden eyes seemed to be set in worshipful purpose, while its mouth was ready to burst into song should the image be suddenly animated to life.

With a single flap of his wings, the Dawn Star rose to become level with the image. He peered closely at it, absorbing every detail.

"It's me," he said finally.

"Yes."

"I'm singing. I mean, the picture looks to be singing just like I do."

"Yes. That is why I made you, to sing and to teach the work of My hands to sing."

"What am I?" The Dawn Star swept his arms, indicating the images on the wall. "What are we all?"

"You are of a race of beings called angels," answered the One. "In all that is yet to be, there will be none like you. You will belong to the heavenly realms. You will all be emissaries to My creation. And you, My Dawn Star, are one of but a few. You are an archangel."

The Dawn Star smiled at the name as if he were being given a great honor, but it had no more meaning to him then the word *angel* did. What he knew for certain was that he was the Dawn Star, and he could sing and had been given charge over a beautiful tree that grew songs, and he was in the presence of the One. Nothing seemed more significant than that.

"What is an archangel?" he asked.

"One with whom I will share a great gift."

"Like the tree of songs?" the Dawn Star asked.

The One smiled. "Yes, and much more."

Before the Dawn Star could ask the question forming on his lips, the One gestured to him. "Come and sit here," He said, indicating a place in the middle of the floor in front of and away from the raised dais. "Wait here and watch."

The One walked to the dais. As the Dawn Star watched Him from his newly assigned station on the temple floor, He reascended to the dais and His throne of glory. Though he was not directly beside the One, the Dawn Star felt as if the One were still very close to him even as He sat upon His throne, high and elevated. It was one of the great mysteries of the One, the sensation of being close to Him, as close as his own breath, even closer than that, but at the same time able to observe the One's actions at a distance. He could see the bold, deliberate movements of the One but could not discern the details.

The One looked to be in a conversation, one to which the Dawn Star was not privy, a conversation with Himself. The three that made up the One spoke at different turns, and each listened intently to the other. The Dawn Star then saw part of the One, which he was coming to know as the Father, throw His head back in a loud thunderous laugh and then quickly nod as if to indicate a hearty agreement with whatever was suggested by this "Committee of the Divine."

When the meeting of the three in the One came to an end, the One stood upon His throne as his glory became brighter and even more abundant. Though it was difficult to see through the brightness, the Dawn Star observed the One reaching into the great crown of glory above Him and collecting from it a great ball that He now held in front of Him.

After observing it for a while, the One began to pat the ball and squeeze it gently with his hands. He was shaping it into something of His own design. The Dawn Star had no discernible idea about what it could possibly be. As the One patted, squeezed, and shaped His own glory, the brightness gradually began to subside until a distinct visible finished creation lay gently cradled in the arms of the One. The Dawn Star looked on in reverent awe as the One held the being close to His breast and gently rocked it. It appeared to be a creature of light like himself, with arms and legs that could not be contained completely in the arms of the One, made from the glory of God.

The Dawn Star looked on as the One rose from His throne and descended to the floor of the temple, carrying the new creation securely until He gently laid it on the floor. The Dawn Star watched from a distance as the One leaned down to kiss its head and whispered something in its ear.

The Dawn Star wondered if the drama he had just seen play out had been performed for the first time, or was he seeing a repeat of how he himself had come to be in the company of the One? Had he, the Dawn Star, been created from the glory of God as well? His thoughts were interrupted when the creature on the floor opened its eyes and stood on its strong, powerful legs for the first time. He remembered his own beginning and the words of the One telling him that he was the first of a great host. Now it seemed the heavenly host was coming into being with this new addition.

The one who stood at the Lord's whispered command glowed liked burnished bronze. He stood a head taller than the Dawn Star and was wider across the shoulders than his golden counterpart. His hairless head gleamed like a dark round jewel in the light of the temple. The Dawn Star smiled at what he saw and spoke his quiet approval: "Beautiful."

As if in response, the bronze creation threw his head back and laughed with boisterous delight very reminiscent of the Father's laugh. Still laughing, he began to run around the One, circling him faster and faster until he became a bright bronze blur. The laughter, now combined with the Dawn Star's and the One's, echoed off the walls of the temple and filled it as if it had physical substance and surrounded them.

The blur slowed into the form of the bronze creation. As he came to a full stop, he threw his hands into the air, sighed deeply, and fell backward into the engulfing arms of the One. The Dawn Star closed his eyes and smiled as he relived again the first time he was similarly engulfed; there was no place he would rather be than in the deep, close presence of the One. He opened his eyes to a conversation between the new arrival and the One. The words remained between the two of them until he heard the One speak the name Michael as the new creature pointed to himself. With that, Michael flung himself into the arms of the One and hugged Him deeply.

Coming away from the embrace, Michael looked around to take in his surroundings. When he saw the Dawn Star sitting at a distance, he pointed a finger and shouted with joy, "Who's that?"

Before the One could answer, Michael ran toward the Dawn Star, leaped, and caught him around the waist just as he stood to make his escape from the oncoming force. They tumbled onto the temple floor together in a gold and bronze heap. Michael's laughter accompanied the playful struggle. The Dawn Star managed to extricate himself from Michael's embrace and attempted to fly away from him, who did not yet have wings. But just as he was about to reach a safe altitude, Michael jumped and caught the Dawn Star by the ankle.

"Hey! Come back here!" He laughed.

He pulled the Dawn Star back down to the floor and continued the benevolent mauling. They played and tumbled together on the floor of God's temple until the One drew near and picked them both up into his arms, where they rested with the Dawn Star on His right and Michael on His left.

"Michael, this is Lucifer, the Dawn Star," said the One. "And this is Michael."

They both smiled at each other and said in chorus, "We've met." Then there was a great explosion of laughter, which brightened the room even more.

When their laughter faded into an echo, the One gently set His bundle onto the floor, where they stood facing each other. They looked at one another and were fascinated by what they saw. The Dawn Star reached up and patted Michael's muscular shoulders and looked into his copper eyes. With one of his large brown hands, Michael gently caressed the Dawn Star's wing, which undulated behind him. Besides their individual colors, the two were very different. Where the Dawn Star moved with a light, easy grace as if he were one with the very air that surrounded them, Michael was strong and deliberate in his movements, which disguised a secret gentleness as demonstrated in the way he ran his fingers through the Dawn Star's hair. Michael touched his own smooth scalp and laughed as if it were a joke that only he understood.

As they stood together admiring each other's beauty, they turned and looked to the One and said, "Thank you," for it seemed as if they were a gift to each other from God, which in a way they were.

In this moment with the One and Michael, a song the Dawn Star had picked from the tree of songs came into his mind. When he had first learned it, he had not understood its meaning. But now, surrounded by the images of the host on the temple walls, it was all clear to him, so he sang a hymn of the heavenly host and the glory of God.

His voice swelled and resounded off the walls. He slowly lifted off the floor as he continued to sing. The glory of God swelled brighter with every note and chorus. Though the Dawn Star was high above the temple floor, he never was above the glory of the One, for it seemed that nothing could diminish the Lord in height or breadth. Below him,

Michael danced around the One with his arms outstretched and his knees lifting high in great giant steps.

When the song was finished, the Dawn Star was welcomed back down to the floor with a big embrace from Michael.

"What was that?" he said. "What were you doing?" It seemed as if he would burst with excitement.

"I was singing," the Dawn Star replied. "I was singing a song."

"Singing a song?"

"It's called music," the One added.

"Oh, I like music!" came Michael's enthusiastic reply. "Where did the music come from?"

Before the Dawn Star could tell him about the tree of songs, the One said, "I gave it to him, and the Dawn Star is going to give it to you."

"Yes!" said the Dawn Star, brightening. "Yes, it would give me great joy to share this gift with you." He turned and faced Michael and sang part of the refrain from the hymn of the heavenly host. When he stopped, he said, "Now do you hear it in your head?"

Michael paused as if listening to something far off in the distance. Then his face brightened, and he pointed to his head and said, "Yes! I hear it!"

"Good," the Dawn Star replied. "Now let it come out here."

With a golden finger, he touched Michael's mouth. Almost at once the notes of the simple refrain came forth from Michael's lips, supported on the tones of a bright baritone voice. It was followed immediately by a great guffaw of laughter. The Dawn Star and the One laughed with him.

"This is one my favorites!" the Dawn Star said as he began to sing the temple song.

He was soon joined by Michael, who sang each note with him

word-for-word. They continued singing together as they danced around the One, Michael with his great steps and bounds and the Dawn Star gracefully leaping and twirling. When the song was complete, they both found themselves directly in front of the One.

Michael looked at Him breathless. There was no movement or words. He simply stood and took in the immense, mysterious, awesome beauty of the One as if he were seeing it all for the first time.

"O Lord my God," escaped from his lips finally.

Then he did what only seemed natural for him to do in the moment; he knelt and worshipped the One. The Dawn Star knew what Michael was experiencing at this moment, for he himself had been caught in a tidal wave of overwhelming emotion when it came to love and adoration of the One. Caught in it again, the Dawn Star found himself alongside Michael, bowing before the Lord his God.

They continued to worship as the One moved back and up to the raised dais. The Dawn Star added to the worship experience by singing again the song of the heavenly host and the glory of God. Michael joined him when more of the hymn became familiar to him. As before, the glory of the One grew brighter and swelled around Him during the song.

When it came to an end, the One stood upon His throne and again began to speak to the essence of who He was. Michael stood behind the Dawn Star with one big arm resting on his shoulders and asked, "Who is he talking to?"

The Dawn Star smiled as he recalled the meeting that preceded Michael's creation and said simply, "Himself."

In this conference, it was the Son who seemed to be the prominent voice amid the gathering. At one point, the Son raised His hand to His mouth and brought it away with His palm turned upward. In His hand, which now extended out in front of Him, was a small orb of light reminiscent of the glory that was all around the One. The ball of glory began to grow as the Son spoke to it. The Dawn Star could not discern the specific words but could hear the low comforting tones that came forth from Him. The voice flowed smoothly, and the light grew bigger with each word until it took the shape of a being with its legs and arms curled up and cradled close to the breast of the One.

The Dawn Star smiled and wondered at his own beginning. What personality of the One was behind his coming into being? Was he shaped like Michael? Was he spoken into life like the silver image that now slept in the arms of the One? As these questions hung in his mind, the One stepped from His throne, cradling the new arrival. As with Michael, He carried it gently down to the floor of the temple. The being lay safely in the One's arms as if it had always been part of Him.

With every aspect of this new one's creation, Michael expressed his overall wonder with a steady stream of vowel sounds, "oh, ooh, ah," punctuated by an occasional short, guttural "hm." The Dawn Star smiled at his responses as they were spoken into his ear. Having just witnessed the sheer wonder of Michael's creation, he could appreciate what Michael was feeling for the first time.

As the One laid the silver creation on the temple floor, the Dawn Star and Michael leaned in, breathless and quiet as they waited for what unfolded next. The One leaned over the new being, who lay sleeping on his side with his arms and legs curled up to his chest and chin, and whispered something into his ear. The Dawn Star and Michael could only imagine what was spoken to the creation on the floor as they watched his eyes flutter open and turn to face the source of the words. Upon finding the face of the One looking at him, the silver being reached out a long arm and touched His face. As the One straightened, the new being—with his hand still on His face—flowed up with Him to his full height.

He was not quite as tall as Michael but more so than the Dawn Star. Though still muscular, Gabriel, was quite a bit leaner than the both of them. The light of the temple and glory reflected off his skin in silver and blue undulations. His short hair came to a peak like the white tips of a cresting wave.

The response from the two witnesses was a quiet and in unison: “Beautiful.”

Michael and the Dawn Star watched the One take the hand of silver from His face and hold it out from Him like the beginning of dance between two partners. While they held each other’s hand, the new creation and his creator started a dance that began with them slowly walking around each other and gradually moving into the precise steps of a choreography that was known only to the two dancers. Soon the One led the new creation into a waltz that covered most of length of the temple.

They orbited Michael and the Dawn Star quite a few times as the two looked on in awe and wonder.

“I ran,” Michael said as he watched the couple flow around the room.

“I spun and leaped,” the Dawn Star replied.

“What?” Michael questioned as he turned to look at him.

The Dawn Star smiled and said, “It was fun.”

The dance came to an end. The new one stood quiet and still in front of the One until suddenly he crouched, jumped, and dove into the presence of the One with his arms extended out from his body. Having experienced it once and now seeing it again for the second time, the Dawn Star smiled at the sheer joy of being engulfed in the presence of the One as he watched the silver being get lost in His arms.

“I wonder who he is,” Michael said.

"I think we're about to find out," the Dawn Star said as he watched the new one speak to the One while seated in the crook of his arm.

The subject of the conversation, which they could not hear, became clear when the silver one pointed to himself and the One said just loud enough so they could hear, "Gabriel." He leaned forward and kissed the newly christened Gabriel upon the head.

From his perch in the One's arm, Gabriel looked out and discovered the gold and bronze duo looking on in fascination. He climbed smoothly down from where he sat and stood on the floor in front of the One, facing them as they moved toward him, Michael with his long strides and the Dawn Star hovering just above the floor with the aid of his wings. Upon his arrival, with a great big laugh, Michael picked Gabriel up in his big arms and jostled him up and down. Gabriel smiled in surprised joy at this exuberant greeting.

The Dawn Star hovered above them both and saw Michael look up at him with a playful gleam in his eye. Without a second's pause, Michael effortlessly tossed Gabriel to the Dawn Star, who caught him under his arms and soared him up into the lofty heights of the temple. The Dawn Star held a good grip on his charge until he caught the eye of the One, who was smiling when He said, "Now to me!" He held His arms wide open.

The Dawn Star gave Gabriel a quick swing before letting go, which sent him somersaulting directly into the waiting arms of the One. Gabriel landed with a squeal of glee at the center of God's glory. The Dawn Star followed suit, diving headfirst to the same place. Soon Michael was tangled up with them after springing from the floor into the presence of the One.

All three found themselves caught up in His arms. They looked at one another, admiring each other as well as the One, who had made them. They felt a new sense of wholeness with Gabriel's arrival. To the Dawn Star it was the understanding of being even more complete.

The One spoke their names as He looked at each of them with great love: "Gabriel, Michael, Lucifer …" He set them down in front of Him and continued, "You are the first of a great host. With you I will establish the fullness of the kingdom of heaven. You shall be the heralds of my strength"—He looked directly at Michael—"My word"—His gaze moved to Gabriel—"and My praise." He looked last at the Dawn Star.

"You shall lead my host according to My will," He said to all of them. "You shall have authority over all that is given to you. I am the One who has spoken this to you. Besides Me, there is nothing that can or will undo what I the Lord your God has decreed."

As the One spoke to them, He seemed to grow in majesty and might. The mystery that the Dawn Star had experienced before from the One became more prevalent. It was the revelation that he would never fully know all there was to know of the One. Only the love that came from the One seemed to be the constant that connected the mystery, majesty, wonder, and glory of God together. His great love was what bound the Dawn Star, Michael, and Gabriel together, and together as they stood, knelt, and bowed before the One, they worshipped Him … and the Dawn Star sang.

IN THE PALACE AGAIN

When the final notes of the song echoed a way, they remained still and silent. The quiet of the moment bathed them in peace. The first sound to gradually infiltrate the silence was a quiet "thank you" spoken by Gabriel, who was on his knees facing the One. Michael rose from his bowed position and stood with the Dawn Star. They looked at one another and then to the kneeling Gabriel, who they had just heard speak for the first time.

They smiled and watched him until he completed his meditation before the One. The four of them stood together in the temple, framed by the glory of God, for a long while until Gabriel looked at them, sighed deeply, and said, "Hello."

After a beat, they all burst into laughter together. That led into the Dawn Star and Gabriel being engulfed in the great arms of Michael as the One looked on in delight at his three archangels playing together.

"Come. I have much to show you," said the One as He began to walk toward the great open doors of the temple.

The three followed Him out and found Him waiting for them on the threshold, just before the great staircase. Before them was the vista of golden mist and clouds that hid much of the city of God.

The Dawn Star stood beside the One as Michael and Gabriel crossed the threshold from the left and the right and took in as much of the golden vista as they could. Michael became fascinated with the structures of the city of God that appeared from the cloudy mist and were quickly covered up just as he was about to point them out.

"Look! What is that? Wait it's gone … No! There it is again!"

He was so taken with the mystery hidden in the clouds that he got on his knees and peered over the edge to get a closer look.

The Dawn Star, Gabriel, and the One moved closer until they stood over him as he searched the mysteries of the golden mist. The Dawn Star was not exactly sure how Michael fell off the platform, whether he was leaning too far or was nudged into the plunge by a gentle push from the One, but he fell with a loud burst of surprised laughter and disappeared beneath the golden mist.

Almost immediately, a ball of light shot forth from the One's hand and followed the same trajectory as Michael. A flash of light revealed itself beneath the mist. Then a bolt of Michael emerged with two great wings spreading out from between his shoulders. He soared above them. His great, boisterous laughter accompanied his flight, even as he landed heavily on the threshold with a *thump.*

The Dawn Star smiled as he recalled the moment in the palace of all things when he had received a similar gift. With that memory, his own wings undulated in reflex and lifted him above the floor a few feet as he watched Michael fling himself at the One in a mauling embrace. The One received it with gracious joy.

As all this unfolded, Gabriel stood and watched in silent glee, which had begun the moment Michael had exited the platform. His eyes went wide in surprise, and his hands clapped over his mouth to suppress an exclamation of surprise or laughter. His silent laughter continued with his shoulders pumping rapidly up and down. So caught up in the humor of the events surrounding Michael getting his wings, he became unaware of his own proximity to the edge. A wayward step backward resulted in his own rapid exit from the platform.

As with Michael, light from the One followed Gabriel, and out of the bright burst, he rose, carried by two great wings of his own. As he floated back up to the threshold of the temple, the Dawn Star could see his shoulders still moving up and down in laughter, even as his eyes were squeezed tightly shut. His silent glee continued even as he landed on the threshold. His laughter ended with a great heave of his shoulders and loud exhalation of air ending in a falsetto *whoof.*

Michael and the Dawn Star gathered around Gabriel and were admiring his new acquisitions when the voice of the One refocused their attention.

"Come with me," He said as He began to walk down the great staircase.

The trio immediately made to follow the One, but they stopped short at the top step as they gazed down at what was laid out below them.

The mist that had covered the stairs during the Dawn Star's first descent with the One had completely dissipated, and the entire staircase as well as the palace of all things was in full, glorious view. The rest of God's city that surrounded them remained a shrouded golden mystery.

But to the Dawn Star, there was no longer any mystery about the palace of all things. His only memory of the palace's exterior was of the great jade doors that he had entered with the One. Now from his vantage point at the top of the stairs, he saw it all.

When the Dawn Star had been inside the palace, it was still and quiet, permanent and steadfast. In contrast, the bright opalescent exterior of the building seemed more like a living organism, for it was in constant motion. Walls constructed themselves and formed a new wing even as they stood and watched. Minarets and towers grew like a blooming thing from the corners. What started out as a simple window multiplied into a dozen or expanded into one with many panes of colored glass winking light back to them. The whole structure was living and active.

The only things that remained unchanged from the outside were the great jade doors and the top of the great tower that the Dawn Star had ascended with the One in order to view the holy temple. The palace moved and changed while the doors and the tower remained unchanged and immovable.

The Dawn Star watched the palace as it grew and developed. Each new addition seemed as if it had always belonged there. The palace never looked unfinished or seemed incomplete; it was just more complete. He looked at Michael and Gabriel and thought to himself, *Just like I am with them.*

Michael broke the silence, pointing down to the palace. "What is that?"

"The palace of all things," said the One, continuing His descent down the stairs.

"It moves …" said Michael.

"It's growing …" Gabriel said quietly.

"Because all things are possible," came the reply of the One.

The Dawn Star thought of the many doors and corridors he had seen when he visited the palace the first time. He smiled and said quietly to himself, "Many possibilities," as the company flew, floated, and walked down the golden staircase toward the living palace below them.

Once again, the Dawn Star found himself in front of the great doors with the One by his side. Michael flew above and behind them, watching the drama of the building. His arms and legs moved as he attempted to duplicate the actions of the palace.

Gabriel stood at the doors and stared at them pensively. Just as the Dawn Star had once done. Gabriel then ran his fingers over the unknown designs etched into the doors. His fingers gracefully danced over them, lightly touching each arc and line. His head was bowed, and his eyes were closed in concentration as if he were listening for a far-off sound.

As his hand passed over a series of letters, his lips moved in silence until he said softly, "In My love and in My glory." He then looked at the One and pointed at Him. "In Your love and in Your glory."

"Yes," said the One.

The Dawn Star immediately understood this to be the meaning of the symbols inscribed upon the doors of jade. It was simple in form and meaning, but there was nothing about the palace of all things that was simple to the Dawn Star. Having been inside and having been shown firsthand the wonders of the room of readiness, the room of God's word, and his beloved tree of songs, and now having witnessed the palace grow without taking up any more space, he could attest to the non-simplicity of it all.

To the Dawn Star, the palace was a mystery in purpose and design. Though some of it was revealed to him, he understood in part, not in whole. There was still so much to learn and discover. Perhaps that was the point of the words on the doors. The love and glory of the One were a wondrous mystery that drew one in to experience and explore its many facets, which were never revealed at once; rather, each discovery created the desire for more.

He looked up at the face of the One, who looked at him in turn, seeming to know his thoughts and affirming his silent musings with a simple smile.

As the One looked at the Dawn Star, the jade doors swung slowly open. Michael descended and stood with them on the threshold. The image of the heart star designed into the floor greeted them as they walked along its longest point.

When they stood at the center of the heart star and subsequently the middle of the great hall, the Dawn Star stood closer to the One and took His hand as if to indicate a shared familiar secret between two friends. He smiled at Michael and Gabriel as they took in the overwhelming sight of the great hall, no doubt perplexed a bit by the static stillness of the interior in contrast to the constant kinesics of the palace's exterior.

At first only their heads turned and pivoted and they stayed close to the One and the Dawn Star, but eventually they walked around them and used their wings to take in as much as they could without straying too far away from the center.

Michael and Gabriel returned to the group simultaneously, their attention drawn to the sets of closed doors on the left- and right-hand sides of the hall. These were the doors to the room of readiness and the room of God's word. Michael looked to the amber-colored doorway as Gabriel's gaze was captured by the emerald doorway.

The Dawn Star only looked forward toward the doors of amethyst, which were partially open, allowing the soft light from the room behind them to spill out onto the polished floors through the narrow opening. He smiled as he closed his eyes to recall the memories of the tree of songs.

In his mind he came upon a song he had learned from before. At first the jaunty tune and the words that went with it had no meaning to him, for it told of a place that stood and moved and where love and glory abounded. Though he had enjoyed learning and singing it, the song had no reference for him until now. He now knew it was the song for the palace of all things.

When the memory of the song came into the Dawn Star's head, the One began to clap out a slow, steady rhythm: *clap, clap, clap, clap.* The Dawn Star opened his mouth and began to sing.

While He continued to clap, the One instructed Michael to begin a faster counter-rhythm that involved stamping his feet and clapping, which Michael did with his usual boisterous enthusiasm: *Stamp, stamp, clap, clap. Stamp, stamp, clap, clap.*

Gabriel began twisting his body from left to right in time to the music. In doing so, his wings, which were stretched out horizontally from his body, made a low humming whooshing sound as they cut through the air.

Whoosh, whoosh.

Clap, clap, clap, clap.

Clap, clap, stamp, stamp.

Whoosh, whoosh.

Amid this percussion, the Dawn Star sang. He sang with joy swelling up within him and pouring out into his singing.

He sang as the heavenly company kept time and danced in the hall of the palace of all things.

He sang and his golden body grew brighter.

He sang and the wonders of the palace, its steadfast interior and its ever-changing exterior, became more vivid in his mind.

He sang and the glory of the One overwhelmed them all, surrounding them, filling them, uniting them all together in His deep mysterious love. This was the reason and the purpose for the palace of all things, as inscribed upon the great jade doors, synthesized and summarized in this moment with the three archangels of heaven being engulfed in the love and glory of the One.

When the song ended and the great hall was still and silent again, the three archangels each found themselves standing in front of one of the three doorways, which were all now wide open. Michael stood looking into the room of readiness. Gabriel did the same before the room of God's word. The Dawn Star had eyes only for the tree of songs with its glowing fruit.

The glory of the One had so filled the width and breadth of the room that, though they were separated from each other, each archangel was aware of the One standing with him. The Dawn Star looked around for Gabriel and Michael and observed that the three entities that made up the One had become more distinct as individuals as the angels stood before the three rooms. It was clear that the Father was standing with Michael, and the Son stood with Gabriel. It was the Spirit who stood with him.

The Three that made up the One were all distinct in personality and character. The Father and the Son seemed more similar to one another. The Spirit, however was the most unique of the Three, almost a completely different creature altogether, more feminine, if the Dawn Star was able to make that distinction, but still part of the Completeness of God.

The next sound to enter the stillness was spoken by the Father and the Son simultaneously. The Dawn Star smiled as he remembered how he felt his first time in the palace of all things when he heard the One say to him, as He now said to Gabriel and Michael, "Come and see."

With that invitation, Michael followed the Father into the room of readiness, and Gabriel followed the Son into the room of God's word. The Dawn Star could only imagine their reactions as they each took in the wonders of those rooms. Having experienced them both, he was more than content to be once again reunited with his beloved tree.

With the Spirit accompanying him, the Dawn Star walked into the room and flew up to one of the middle branches. He stood on the limb and looked up and around at the multitude of soft lights that grew from them. He pressed his hand flat against the tree's trunk as if to balance himself as his head swiveled around to take in every detail. Immediately the Dawn Star felt a low hum move through his palm and eventually to other parts until his entire body resonated with the tone of the tree.

He took his hand away, and the hum faded. He touched the trunk again, and it returned, filling him completely. When he removed his hand a second time and the hum resided, the Spirit said, "Leave it."

The Dawn Star returned his hand to the tree's trunk and let the hum fill him again. It wasn't long before a new song with new images entered his mind. Unlike the songs that came from the fruit and burst into his heart and mind like fireworks, the song from the tree took its time to reveal itself.

The low tone moved through him like a river with new notes, melodies, and harmonies flowing into it like tributaries. With these additions, the story and the song of the tree began to reveal itself in the Dawn Star's mind.

He saw the One standing in the great hall. Only the image of the heart star on the floor revealed it to be the great hall because it was empty of all else. Except for the Three that made up the One, He was alone, but He was not lonely. The One stood in a space near the top point of the heart star and began singing.

When the Dawn Star had heard the One sing for the first time, it had been with a singular voice and a singular melody. Now he heard the One sing a song in close three-part harmony that filled his body even more than the tree's singular hum. He did not understand the words, but it did not seem to matter.

As the song within a song continued, the Dawn Star observed one of the tiny constellations that orbited the One's heart make its way to His mouth. He caught it in His hand as it emerged from His lips. He then took the tiny light and cradled it gently between the thumb and fingers of His other hand. He then knelt and placed the constellation on the floor of the hall and backed away to stand in the middle of the heart star's image, all the while singing the song in three parts.

The Dawn Star saw the tiny constellation sink and disappear beneath the floor as the One continued to sing. For much time nothing happened except the continuation of the song. There was no way to measure how long the One stood there singing before a small bright green bud revealed itself from the floor. It was so delicate in nature, it seemed that a mere breath could wipe it from existence.

But the song continued, and the bud slowly grew and became stronger but no less delicate in its features. When it grew to a certain height, glowing orbs of light began to emerge among the developing branches. Immediately the Dawn Star understood with joy that the song he was hearing and seeing was about the creation of the tree of songs. He watched the tree grow before his eyes, with new fruit ripening at every new length.

The One continued to sing until the tree reached its final tremendous height. The Dawn Star then watched as the walls of the palace of all things enclosed around it to create for the tree its own chamber. From the song playing in his head, he saw the One set the amethyst doors in place and close them to seal the room, where the tree of songs waited for them to be opened again. With the closing of the amethyst doors, the images faded and the tree song returned to a singular hum.

As he took his hand from the tree's trunk, the humming subsided. The Dawn Star sat down on the limb and sighed with satisfaction.

The Spirit sat beside him and said, "You sang it beautifully."

"What do you mean?" the Dawn Star asked.

"The song of this tree. It was beautiful."

"Was I singing?"

"Every note," the Spirit answered. "I saw the whole thing as you sang it, and I should know because I was there when it happened."

The Dawn Star smiled and shrugged. "I didn't know I was singing. I just saw it all in my head."

"A song can be like that. It can burst forth from the singer without them realizing they are giving it life," the Spirit said.

"Is that how the tree of songs began?" the Dawn Star asked.

"Yes," the Spirit replied. "It was the first of the palace's wonders. Before strength was forged or a word was written, praise was sown and planted in this place. It has been safeguarded behind those doors until you came. It was waiting for you."

The Dawn Star sat silent, pondering what he had just been told about the tree, his tree.

"The tree was the first," he said finally, "as I was the first." This realization made him feel more bound to the tree than he already was.

The Spirit smiled and responded with a soft yes.

The Dawn Star thought again about what he had just witnessed regarding the beginning of the tree of songs. He recalled again the loving, gentle hands of the One holding the seed of light and the One singing as He watched over what had just been planted and how the song and vigil continued until the tree had grown to its maturity.

These images took the Dawn Star's memory back to the holy temple of the One, where he had witnessed the beginning of two others, Michael and Gabriel. It prompted a question that had never been far away from his curiosity since that time.

"How was I made?"

The Dawn Star had the look and countenance of a formidable creature in strength, power, and great beauty. The glory that shone around him was only less so than that of the One's. However, the question he had asked in a small timid manner seemed out of place considering from where it had come. Why should he care? He was here now in the company of the One. He had been given a great gift in the tree of songs. How he was made shouldn't matter. But it did … and he wanted to know. He wanted to know, was he shaped like Michael by the Father, or was he spoken into being by the Son like Gabriel? He wanted to know how he was made.

"You were mine," came the Spirit's gentle reply. "Let me show you."

The Spirit touched the Dawn Star gently on the forehead, and the scene immediately changed to that of the temple, where he saw the One upon the raised dais. He recognized that the Three were in conversation with each other, something he had witnessed twice before prior to the births of Michael and Gabriel.

When all was said between the Three, the Holy Spirit became more prominent and began to sing in a bright contralto voice. As the song was being sung, glory poured out of the Spirit's mouth and rose above the One's head. The Dawn Star mused that if this was indeed his beginning, he and the tree of songs shared an even deeper connection, for they had both been born from a song.

The Spirit's song continued, and the glory came forth and rose until the song swelled to a dramatic climax at the Spirit's last note, which was held for a multitude of beats. Upon the song's conclusion, the glory that had gathered high above the One's head suddenly burst and began to rain down upon the throne of God.

With joyful glee and arms wide open, the Three in One caught each drop of glory as it fell. There was not one drop that passed the waiting arms. The Lord gathered each droplet close to the breast as they formed into a singular shape. When the showers had ceased, a golden figure with golden locks of hair rested peacefully in the loving arms of the One.

The Dawn Star took in a quick breath as he watched the image of the One lean in to kiss the golden figure on its head. "It's me," he said.

"Yes," said the Spirit. "That is how you came to be."

"With a song."

"Yes," the Spirit agreed. "The song of the Dawn Star." She said with a smile.

The image of the One cradling the golden figure faded, and the Dawn Star sat quietly with the Spirit in the limbs of the tree of songs.

"Thank you," the Dawn Star said … and the Spirit smiled.

THE BELOVED

The Dawn Star sat peacefully with the Spirit in the tree's branches. The soft enigmatic music from the tree accompanied their silence.

A glowing piece of fruit hanging just above them caught the Dawn Star's eye. It was not as large as the other globes, which hung in abundance. It was smaller by half and looked as if it could fit completely in one of the Dawn Star's hands. Along with its size, there was a fragility about it that distinguished it even more from the others. He reached up and touched it lightly with tips of his fingers. There was a warmth about it, not so much in temperature but more as it related to a feeling, similar to what the Dawn Star experiences with the One, but it had more to do with the understanding that this small glowing object or what it represented was loved, deeply.

He made to take his hand from the fruit when the Spirit of the One moved into the Dawn Star's space and surrounded him, sharing it with him.

"May I?" the Spirit asked.

Delighted by this sudden intimacy with the Spirit, the Dawn Star nodded his approval. With the Spirit guiding and leading him, he once again lifted his hand toward the diminutive ball of light. With the Dawn Star's hand in the hand of the Spirit, he took hold of the fruit and gently tugged it free from the tree.

For a while he looked at the small globe resting in his hand while his hand rested in the Spirit's. Then, as he had done when he first sat in the branches of the tree of songs with the One, he gently inhaled the fragrance of the small fruit. As before, the light dissipated as he breathed it in. The Dawn Star smiled at the familiar sensation of the fragrance of light rushing through him, filling his entire being, and settling in his center, and his mind opening to the song it brought to him.

When the song was suddenly revealed to the Dawn Star, he inhaled quickly in an audible gasp, as if the intense feelings contained in the song would overwhelm him. The Spirit held him closer to reassure and steady him as he experienced the flood of emotions contained in the words and structure of the song, which he now understood to be the song of the beloved.

"Shh," the Spirit said to him gently. "You can sing it."

The Dawn Star closed his eyes and waited until there was a reprieve from the onslaught of overwhelming emotion. When that moment came, he began to sing.

The first notes of the song came out in a barely audible falsetto with long sustained notes that ascended the scale in varying intervals. It was a lullaby, a hymn, a love song. It was as if he were singing about something so holy and pure that giving it voice would somehow tarnish its purity … It seemed fragile, delicate but more beautiful than anything he had yet to experience in the kingdom of the One, save for the One Himself.

The song grew gradually in volume as it spoke of a passion between two, the One and the object of the One's affection, the beloved. It was a song of courtship, a dance of splendor between two hearts that longed for each other and came together in holy completion.

As the Dawn Star sang, he came to understand that the song of the beloved had no end; there were only rests and reprieves between verses. Taking the opportunity between one of these reprieves, he asked the Spirit, "Who is the beloved?"

When he asked the question, he heard his voice, but he also heard the voices of the others—specifically Gabriel and Michael—asking the same question at the exact same moment. At the Spirit's beckoning, the Dawn Star descended the tree and walked out toward the center of the great hall just as Michael was coming from the room of readiness and Gabriel from the room of God's word. The Father, the Son, and the Spirit came together as the One at the center of the heart star. The three archangels stood gazing upon the One in renewed wonder with the question still fresh from their lips.

"Who is the beloved?" the One repeated. "Who *are* the beloved," the One said. "Let me show you." With those words, the three joined the One at the center and began to ascend the great hall.

The Dawn Star recalled the first time he had experienced this journey when it was just him and the One. He looked again upon the many doors and corridors that surrounded them at each level of their journey. The One's answer to his question about the doors from the first time echoed in his mind: "When a new possibility is needed." The Dawn Star thought the only possibility he could ever want was what he was experiencing at this moment with Michael, Gabriel, and the One.

As they neared the top of the great hall, the image of the heart star loomed above them. The Dawn Star assumed that this would be their final destination, but they did not pause. When they reached the ceiling, they passed through the image like a veil of mist.

For a moment they were surrounded by nothing but deep dark violet until above their heads a multitude of tiny specks of light burst upon them. The company moved up and through them, and the Dawn Star discovered that they were more than just points of light. He heard faint sounds of laughter generated from high and low voices, brief notes of songs being sung, and snippets of conversations. All faded in and out as they passed by and through them.

"These are the beloved?" Gabriel asked.

"Not entirely," the One answered. "These are my thoughts, designs, and dreams for each one of the beloved, all of them. It is what they will be."

As the One spoke of them, the specks of light swirled more quickly around the archangels and the One, and the sounds they made became more excited.

"Everything in my city, everything in the kingdom of heaven is for them." The One paused and looked at each of His archangels "Even you were ultimately created for the beloved, to serve them, to teach them, to protect them, to inspire them, to guide them into a deeper understanding of My love for them that they may know what you know."

With that word, a wave of affection from the One overwhelmed them as if to remind the three that they were indeed deeply loved by God. It was a sweet reminder of what they had already come to know.

They remained together in that place surrounded by the lights and sounds of the beloved. Wherever they were in the top of the great hall, there seemed to be no end to the violet firmament and, in turn, no end to the tiny specks of light … They were limitless.

Each of the archangels were captivated by the tiny things. Michael extended a big strong hand, and a multitude of them settled into his palm and rested there gently. On the tip of one of Gabriel's fingers, a single point found its place. He brought it close to his face and examined it, studying it as if to learn its every detail.

The Dawn Star made a bowl with his hands to gather some of them. He bent his ear to listen to the sounds they made. He smiled at the snippets of laughter he heard and the songs they sang. He tried to piece a whole tune together to no avail; they were only ideas that were not yet complete. But he was no less delighted by them, as he was with all things musical. As he listened, he thought of the blue ball in the round chamber in the room of God's word. The home of the beloved, the One had said.

The One spoke. "Sing, Dawn Star. Sing."

The Dawn Star understood immediately what the One was telling him. He closed his eyes and began to sing the next verse in the song about the beloved. The intense emotions returned as he sang, which caused him to sing with growing volume and passion.

He opened his eyes to see that Michael and Gabriel were also overcome with emotion. The One had ascended away from them and looked as He did enthroned upon the raised dais in His holy temple.

The Dawn Star gradually became aware that he was no longer singing alone, for the One had added His voice to his own. As they sang together, the points of light began to gather and swirl around the head of the One until it seemed as if all the lights of the beloved in the purple firmament were gathered above Him. They swirled so quickly now, it looked as if the One were wearing an enormous solid crown of light.

For a few verses, they sang together until the Dawn Star could no longer bear to give voice to the intense emotions manifested by the song. He could not endure the intimacy he felt between the beloved and the One. Though they were only the ideas of the beloved, he could only imagine the intensity of emotions between the two when the beloved at last came to be. To continue singing the song felt like an intrusion.

The three archangels closed their eyes to lessen the intensity of the light and emotions. They kept them that way through the duration of a half dozen more verses. Only the Dawn Star was aware that there were an infinite number of verses yet to be sung in the song of the beloved.

When the last note was sung, they opened their eyes and once again found themselves on the floor of the great hall, standing on the image of the heart star. It was as if they had just imagined the entire experience. They seemed out of breath, but as they beheld the One standing in their midst, they felt restored.

Michael spoke first. "My Lord, the beloved, or that which will be the beloved, they moved so quickly around your head."

Gabriel continued the thought, "Like a crown."

The Dawn Star thought again of what was to come … all the images and books in the room of God's word, the bright yellow ball, the blue one that would orbit it—the Earth is what the One called it—all that would be created. An idea suddenly came into his head, and the Dawn Star spoke it.

"The beloved will be the crown of Your creation."

The One looked gently at the Dawn Star and said nothing, but His silence said that it was indeed true.

THE HOST

With thoughts of the beloved still on their minds, the One spoke. "The time of the host is upon us."

The One was standing in the middle of the image of the heart star. His glory began to grow out from Him. It became brighter as it filled the great hall and completely engulfed the three of them. The Dawn Star closed his eyes against its bright intensity. He held his breath, for he felt that if he were to take a breath, it would be more than he could bear.

They were barely aware of the floor disappearing from beneath their feet. With the sound of the One's voice, the intensity of God's glory began to dissipate.

"Prepare to receive your host."

Shortly after, there was a sound of a great deep breath being taken.

The Dawn Star opened his eyes and found that they were back in the temple, hovering high above the floor. The raised dais was below and away from where they were. Gabriel was at His left hand, and Michael was to His right. The Dawn Star hovered a few feet higher than his brother archangels, though it was not intentional on His part. It was how they were arranged when they found themselves back in the temple.

They watched as the One seemed to breath in His own glory and waited as the temple became quiet and still. No one moved or heard any sound.

The Dawn Star could not remember in his brief time with the One when there was nothing to be heard. There had been laughter and singing and whooshing and talking, but now there was a silence so profound it felt like its own entity, like a living part of heaven itself that just now had made itself known.

In that moment of divine quiet, the Dawn Star felt a new sensation of being alive and in the presence of the One. There were no restless thoughts or urges to sing or dance. In the silence between the inhale and the exhale of the One, there was only peace and the contentment to be exactly where he was in this moment, content in the knowledge that what would come next would not take away or diminish the beauty of the holy silence that was discovered in the waiting …

When the exhalation came, it was slow and deliberate, making a sound that was barely heard. The breath of God's glory settled onto the floor like a great blanket of light. It spread itself around the raised dais, which was the throne of the One, completely surrounding it.

Above the temple floor, Gabriel and Michael instinctively moved to position themselves around the One so that there was an equal distance of thirds between the three of them. The Dawn Star maintained his position directly in front of the One with the open temple doors at his back.

The blanket of glory continued to grow thicker until the entire area below the archangels' feet was covered with the visible manifestation of the breath of God. The deep silence returned when the exhalation came to an end. All was still except for slight undulations of the glory resting on the temple floor.

The One stepped down from the dais and looked at the Dawn Star. In that moment, he knew what the One was asking of him. Instinctively he opened his mouth and began to sing the song of the heavenly host.

As the sound of the hymn filled the space, the glory below began to dissipate and form itself into figures that seemed to be kneeling, crouching, or lying curled up on the floor. Before long, Michael added his voice to the first song he had heard in the temple in the company of the Dawn Star and the One.

Gabriel listened intently as his brothers sang. With visual encouragement from the Dawn Star, he began to sing as well. He smiled at the sound of his own tenor voice.

As the three sang together, more and more figures began forming across the floor. The One walked among them, touching each one tenderly, kissing them, caressing them. Upon each encounter with the One, the figures became animated and began to be more distinctive in character and design, like living jewels scattered across the floor of the temple.

As the One moved through the temple, His glory gathered around Him like a swirling robe, catching each figure up into its folds as He passed them. When it seemed that the last figure became part of the robe of glory, the One began to rise from the temple floor.

With each new level, more jewel-like figures appeared in the folds of the robe … layers and layers of heavenly beings with the One at the center. As the One rose higher, the trio of archangels rose with Him. They maintained their equal distance from each other as they traveled through the roof of the temple.

The Dawn Star continued to sing the song of the heavenly host and knew in his heart that the three of them were watching the great host of the Lord being created from the breath and glory of God.

As the One continued His journey even higher, the layers of his robe became too numerous to count as the host multiplied with each new level. Before long, the jeweled host of heaven added itself to the golden vista of the city of God as if it had always been there.

When the song of the heavenly host came to an end, the ascent of the One ceased and the creation of the angelic host was complete.

The Dawn Star surveyed the sight before him. The newly created host circled the One in countless numbers. He recalled the images of the host etched upon the walls of the holy temple; now those images had been given life and were living before him.

They moved about the One in a spiral fashion, which reminded the Dawn Star of the image of a galaxy the One had showed him in the circular chamber when the scroll of the heavens and Earth opened. It was a galaxy of angels with the glory of the One shining large, bright, and full at its center.

The Dawn Star, Michael, and Gabriel maintained their positions on the edge of the mass like three bright shining stars standing vigil as the spiraling host moved in and away from the One at the center. As he watched this new dance, the Dawn Star thought back on the privilege he was given to watch the creation of his brother archangels as well as this vast heavenly host. All of them, now orbiting around the One as one body, had been created from the glory of God. Each one had been sung, shaped, spoken, or breathed into life from the very essence of who God was. All His light, all His love, all His truth were contained in His glory, which was now in all of them.

A question arose in the Dawn Star's thoughts: Did being made from that which made up the essence of the One make them all in a sense one with God or even like God?

Just as the question came to his mind, it was dismissed when he heard the voice of the One speak to him gently as if He were right by his side.

"Go to the Palace and of All Things. Wait for the host there. They will come to you. Receive all who come to you. Show them what I have shown you. Teach them what I have taught you. They will serve you as they serve me."

This last word puzzled the Dawn Star, for he felt no need or desire to be served. His only thought was to be in the presence of the One and to sing the songs that grew in the branches of the tree of songs. The words of the One continued as if to bring clarity.

"Teach them to sing, Dawn Star. Teach them the songs that grow in the tree. By their singing they will serve you as they serve me."

He remembered when he had first sat in the branches of the tree of songs with the One, when he was first told of the host and the heavenly chorus he would lead. He looked at the swirling mass of angels with the One at their center and imagined each and every one of their voices lifted in song to His glory. He was filled with joy as if he could hear them singing already.

Now that time had come, and he would lead them.

Upon receiving the instructions from the One, the Dawn Star made his way back to the palace of all things to wait for his host. Gabriel and Michael joined him, having received similar instructions. As the trio walked into the great hall, they became aware of the three sets of doors standing wide open to the rooms they once enclosed. To their right, they observed the kinetic activity of the room of God's word compared to the gleaming serenity of the room of readiness.

With a passing glance to the rooms on his left and right, the Dawn Star walked in the direction of the soft light spilling out from the room where the tree of songs waited for him. When he walked through the open amethyst doors and stood before the tree, he became aware of his brothers standing just behind him and looking up into the branches. The three stood silently as they took in the tree's majesty.

"What is this?" Michael asked.

"It's called a tree …" Gabriel said.

The Dawn Star smiled, having experienced the room of God's word with its swirling images. Gabriel, no doubt, would have knowledge of trees.

"…a magnificent tree," continued Gabriel.

The Dawn Star said, "It is the tree of songs."

They continued to stand there in silence, taking in the sights and the sounds of the tree, until the Dawn Star, with a simple flap of his wings, began to ascend to and up through the tree. He glanced down to indicate for his brothers to follow him.

They traveled to the middle of the tree and alighted on a branch surrounded by glowing fruit. Michael and Gabriel careened their necks around to try to see everything they could.

The Dawn Star spoke. "This is where the songs I sing come from."

With that, he reached up and gently picked the light fruit closest to him. He held it in both hands for a moment until Michael and Gabriel observed him bring it to his nose and inhale deeply. The Dawn Star smiled at the familiar sensation of the dissipating light filling him until the song it contained revealed itself to him.

What he saw in his heart and mind wasn't just a single song but a series of songs, all connected together to tell a singular story of celebration and praise. What the Dawn Star gave voice to, with Michael and Gabriel looking on, was the main melodic theme of the piece. The entire work would need a multitude of singers giving voice to different parts for the piece to be fully realized and experienced … a symphony of voices brought together under one leader, the Dawn

Star. He could see every part in every movement and knew instantly how it should and would be sung.

The tune Gabriel and Michael heard the Dawn Star sing was a song about a completed work and the joy of resting from that work. They both smiled as their brother sang. Their love and appreciation for him could be seen clearly upon their faces.

When the song was complete, the Dawn Star took a deep breath and stood quietly. He kept his eyes closed in the silence as the music echoed in his memory and he saw in his mind how this piece of music would unite all of creation together as one, for the glory of the One.

When he opened his eyes, the Dawn Star observed his brothers eyeing the light fruit around them. "Go on," he said to them. "Pick one."

Michael smiled and reached to select a fruit that hung just above his head, but as he grabbed it, his fingers passed through it as if he were trying to hold the air itself. The light remained intact. Gabriel also tried to touch the fruit but to no avail. His hand passed through it as well.

Puzzled, the Dawn Star reached to grab the same fruit, which came easily away from the tree as all the other light fruit had before it. He looked to his brothers with wonder. He felt almost apologetic for their inability to lay hold of the fruit.

The Dawn Star held out the fruit to them, but Gabriel stopped him with a gesture of his hand.

"This is yours. The tree of songs is for you. This is your gift."

"But I want to share it with you," the Dawn Star replied.

"Teach us that song," Michael said, pointing to the ball of light resting in his hand.

The Dawn Star looked down at the glowing fruit and smiled. If the only way he could share the tree with his brother archangels was through the songs he sang from it, then he would.

The song he sang from inhaling the fruit was a song that spoke of strength, knowledge, and wonder. It had three distinct parts to it. The first was a melodic tune in a lower register that ascended and descended the scale in a steady rhythm for several measures. This was given to Michael to sing. In the second part, Gabriel was given a countermelody in a higher register that matched his tenor range perfectly.

Michael sang of the strength and power of the One, while Gabriel described the lofty nature of all that the Lord knew and how all creation was known perfectly to God. As the two sang their parts, their voices blending perfectly together, the Dawn Star entered the piece with an elaborate combination of word, rhymes, and melody. It was almost three completely different songs that, if sung singularly, would have been beautiful and complete in and of themselves. But when sung together, they became another more complete song like the very character of the One.

The three sang together, clearly enjoying their brotherhood in song. As one they descended from the tree and back down to the floor. Together they walked to the threshold of the chamber. The Dawn Star stopped and stood in the opening of the two amethyst doors. The other two continued on, Gabriel to his left and Michael to his right. When they arrived at the room of knowledge and the room of strength, respectively, they stood in their doorways, facing each other and singing together the entire time.

They delighted in the song filling the great hall and echoing in a way that made it sound as if a whole host was singing instead of just the three of them. This was the sound that greeted the first of the angelic host as they entered the palace of all things.

They came in bunches of a dozen, stood in the middle of the heart star image, and listened to the song of the three archangels. They all listened carefully to each part. After a few moments, they moved to the part of the song and the archangel they were most drawn to. After a while, each of them began singing the song along with the archangels. This pattern was repeated each time another dozen entered the palace.

The Dawn Star watched as each of the host selected a room to walk into. It was clear that they were given a choice of which place to serve. He took note of each one as they approached his chamber doors. Some walked to him, others made their way to where he waited by dancing or skipping, and some floated without benefit of wings. The Dawn Star was curious about this. He noticed the only host with wings were him and his two brothers. Were their wings a symbol of rank or part of their identity as archangels? Were they a gift given by the One to those who would lead? The ultimate reason was left up to the will of the One, which he would accept with whatever responsibility came with it.

As they came, they made their way into the center of the room and stood beneath the outstretched limbs of the tree of songs. Without prompting, some made their way up and through the limbs until almost every part of the tree was filled with the Dawn Star's heavenly host.

When it seemed the last of host had arrived in the palace, the song of the three archangels ended. The last note resonated through the entirety of the great hall. With a smile and a nod to Gabriel and Michael, the Dawn Star turned and entered his chamber, as his brothers did theirs.

The Dawn Star looked up into the tree's branches and marveled at his host filling them, right alongside the glowing fruit. He rose into the tree and joined his host. He greeted them as he passed up through the limbs. Midway through his ascent, he came upon one of his host staring intently at one particular piece of light fruit. The angel was large in girth and height, almost as tall as Michael. He was almost too big for the branch upon which he was seated.

"It's beautiful, isn't it?" the Dawn Star asked.

"Oh yes," the angel replied.

With that, the Dawn Star picked the fruit from the tree and showed it to him.

The angel extended a big hand to receive the fruit but was unable to touch it. His fingers passed through the light. A slight frown began to form on his lips at the realization of his inability to grasp what he desired.

"I think I can help" the Dawn Star said.

He smiled as he looked at the sphere of light resting in the Dawn Star's outstretched hand.

"What is your name?" the Dawn Star asked.

The angel looked up from the fruit, smiled brightly, and chuckled as he said, "The One called me Allegro. I am Allegro."

The Dawn Star smiled. "Allegro, let us see what song you have been given."

He lifted his hand to inhale the fruit and instinctively reached out and took Allegro's hand as he breathed it in. When the familiar sensation began to take effect, he realized the song was revealing itself to both of them at the same time. Allegro's eyes widened in surprise and wonder as the song formed in his mind's eye. He opened his mouth and sang for the first time. Though the Dawn Star knew the song instantly when he inhaled the light fruit and could sing it perfectly if he desired, it was not his to sing. This was Allegro's song to sing and discover.

The song described a creature of delicate beauty with bright patterned wings that fluttered through the air and landed with a whisper. The Dawn Star understood that Allegro's song was that of the butterfly. He remembered it from one of the images he had seen in the room of God's word.

He smiled at the thought of this tiny creature's song being entrusted to one as large as Allegro. His voice stood in stark contrast to his mass as well. It was high and light in register and traveled easily into a falsetto range. His voice seemed to dance as he sung in a gay, upbeat rhythm. His bright blue eyes followed the butterfly's path the song was describing. His meaty fingers drummed lightly upon his great round belly, keeping gentle time as the song progressed.

When the song of the butterfly was complete, Allegro smiled and sighed deeply.

After a moment, the Dawn Star said, "That was very good. You sang it beautifully."

"Thank you. I think I will like singing."

"You are a most welcome addition to my tree." He hadn't necessarily meant to call it "his tree" aloud. But that was how he felt about it. It seemed to be his, especially given the fact that he seemed to be the only one of the host who could physically touch and pick the fruit.

"Your tree?" asked Allegro.

"The tree of songs," said the Dawn Star. "The One entrusted it to me. I am—"

Before he could finish Allegro interrupted him. "I know who you are." He waved his arm in a sweeping motion to indicate the other host. "We all know who you are. The One told us. You are Lucifer, the Light Bringer. You are the Dawn Star." Then in a small voice he asked, "Will you sing my song with me?"

And they sang together.

There was another part of the song the Dawn Star had been given that he added as the song progressed. It described something starting out one way and becoming something else, a new creation from the old. It was about change and great possibility … and beauty.

As he sang with Allegro, the Dawn Star became aware that the host in the tree were gathered around them, listening intently to their song. Everywhere he looked, there was an angel staring back at him. All his host were gathered together in one place around him. What the One had spoken of when he was first given the tree had come to pass. His host were here in the tree with him.

“I want to sing,” said a tall thin angel just above him.

“Teach us to sing, Dawn Star,” said another.

“I want to sing that song,” said an angel, pointing to a light fruit.

And they all began to speak at once, pointing to different pieces of fruit, saying, “What is that song?” and “I want to hear this one …”

One particular piece of fruit caught the Dawn Star’s eye. It hung almost directly above where he and the bulk of his host were located. He rose through the branches in order to reach it. Upon touching it and without knowing why, he instinctively instructed his host to join hands as he took the hand of Allegro, who had followed him up to the light fruit. When all the host in the tree of songs were connected to one another by touch, the Dawn Star picked the fruit from the tree and inhaled its fragrance as he had done so many times before.

The familiar sensation came upon him, but this time it was experienced by his entire host almost at once. In the next moment, with a nod from Dawn Star, the company took a breath in unison and began to sing together in one voice a doxology to the One.

“Praise God from whom all blessings flow …”

GLORIA

Gloria made her way down the golden staircase. She was the last of the angelic host to emerge from the holy temple of the One, who followed close behind her. She stopped after ten stairs, which she had taken one step at a time, placing both feet on each step before moving to the next.

She was the smallest of all the angels. Were she to stand next to Michael, her head would barely reach his chest. Her skin was pearl white, and billows of snowy, curly hair were piled on top of her head. In contrast to her pale features, she had ebony eyes that seemed to take in every detail of whatever she cast her gaze upon, which was now the palace of all things.

Her curls bounced gently as her head followed the movements of the ever-changing exterior of the palace. After a while, her upper body joined in too, swaying left and right, keeping time to the unheard rhythm of the building's constant changes. The One put His hands on her tiny shoulders and moved with her. They continued their journey down the stairs with a single word from Gloria: "Fun." Then she hopped to the next step and then the next and the next until her journey was complete. The One matched her exact movements step for step.

The jade doors of the palace stood wide open when they arrived. Gloria stopped short at the sight of them and the sights and sounds unfolding before her. She stepped back into the One as her big ebony eyes took it all in. She turned to the One and indicated with her hand for Him to bend down so she could say something to Him.

"Where is the tree?" she asked softly.

Bending farther down, the One stretched His hand over her shoulder and pointed to the open amethyst doors directly in front of them.

"Right over there," He said gently.

She took in a sharp breath and then breathed out a soft, excited, elongated "ooh."

"Can I go and see it?" she asked.

"Of course," said the One as He straightened. He took her hand and walked with her across the great hall to where the tree of songs and the host of the Dawn Star were waiting.

As the One and Gloria made their way to the tree, the Dawn Star and his host had begun to sing their doxology to the Lord. This was the sound that greeted them as they stepped into the chamber.

The glory of the One shone brighter as the hymn progressed. Gloria closed her eyes as much to shield them from the brightness as to listen intently to the sound of a multitude of voices singing the song of praise. Her eyes were still closed when the Dawn Star became aware of the One's physical presence with them. Before they came to the end of the piece, the Dawn Star started in again with "Praise God From Whom All Blessings Flow." Soon the host were joining in at different places, turning it into an elaborate canticle with many voices all going in other directions. What at first seemed to be a confusing conglomeration of noise was in actuality an intricate, orderly tapestry of sound bringing praise to God.

Gloria stood with the One, surrounded by His ever-expanding glory. Without a conscious effort, she lifted her arms as if to embrace the very sound filling the chamber. When her hands came into contact with another body, she opened her eyes to find herself among the branches of the tree and in the midst of the host and the doxology filling her mind and soul just as the final amen was being sung by the entire company.

The final notes of the amen were still ringing in the Dawn Star's spirit when a single voice continued an additional amen somewhere below him. It was crystal clear and in the soprano range with a lightness yet to be heard in any of the voices of his host.

The Dawn Star floated down to the branch where Gloria stood just as she finished singing the last note.

"That was beautiful," the Dawn Star said to her.

Until he spoke to her, she was not aware of his presence. She turned and looked into his smiling golden eyes.

"Gloria," the One said. "This is the Dawn Star …"

The Dawn Star smiled at Gloria, and she smiled back at him.

"Hi, Gloria."

"We had a long talk, Gloria and I," said the One. "I told her about the tree of songs, and she wanted to see it for herself. So here we are."

Gloria seemed to be unaware of what the One was saying as her dark eyes took in every detail of the tree of songs and the host, which seemed to fill every branch. She then looked into the eyes of the Dawn Star and studied him for a long time. She took his face into her pearl white hands and brought it close to her own until they were barely two inches apart.

As she peered at him, the Dawn Star glanced up to the One and then returned his gaze to Gloria. He could see his face reflected in her dark eyes.

After a while, the Dawn Star asked, smiling, "What do you see in there?"

"I don't know," she said in a straightforward manner. "Something … and nothing."

The Dawn Star looked from Gloria to the One, questioning her answer. Before the One could speak to his silent inquiry, a shout from Gloria got their attention.

"What's that?" she shouted, pointing to large a light fruit that was easily five times the size of the other fruit.

"Let's find out," the Dawn Star replied.

Leaving the One, he took Gloria by the hand, and the two angels glided to where she was pointing.

Upon arriving to a branch next to the enormous fruit, the Dawn Star said, "This is a song, and from its looks, it is a very big song."

"May I sing it?"

"She's here to help you. There are many songs for all your host to learn. Gloria can help you with that," the One said.

As the One spoke, the Dawn Star picked the large fruit and held it in front of him. Before he could ponder the One's statement further, Gloria reached up and lifted the big ball from his hands and held it as close to her as her arms and the ball's girth would allow.

The Dawn Star was astonished because up to this point he had been the only one who could hold the light fruit as solid objects. All others who had tried had found their hands passing through them as if they were trying to grasp the air. But here was Gloria hugging the fruit, which was so big her head and eyes could barely be seen over the top of the ball of light.

The One said. "To Gloria all praise is tangible as it is to you. It is more than a promise waiting in a tree. It is my glory given voice and body. Praise is not a dream or an illusion. It is real. You and Gloria are able to hold the fruit because you understand that."

"But why her and not the others? Why me?" the Dawn Star asked.

"Your sense of wonder makes it real to you. You and Gloria are creations of my wonder as much as anything else. It is my unique gift to you both."

Before the Dawn Star could ask the questions forming on his lips, the One continued, "Wonder is a gift that is meant to be shared and discovered. If everyone had it, there would be no one to share it with. You and Gloria will share it with your host."

As the One spoke, Gloria continued to stand steadfast, holding onto the great ball.

The Dawn Star looked down at Gloria, who stared back at him unblinkingly. "You are very small," he said.

"Some of my greatest wonder is found in the smallest of things," the One said, smiling at Gloria.

Gloria sighed deeply and raised her ball as high her small arms could stretch. "I want to sing this song."

God and the Dawn Star smiled at one another as he touched the large fruit, leaned down, and made to sniff the light fruit. As he did this, Gloria matched the Dawn Star's every movement so that when he began to inhale the fragrance of the fruit, she breathed it in as well.

As the great ball of light dissipated before them, the image of the song appeared in their minds at the same time. Gloria's eyes grew wide in astonishment at the size of the song. The Dawn Star relished the fragrance with secret joy and delight as he always did when a new song was revealed. They opened their mouths and the Bringer of Light and the smallest of angels sang the new song together.

The lyrics spoke of light and colors, clouds and particles that spread across a great expanse of darkness. They sang of mysteries hidden in mist and beauty that may not be seen but whose beauty would remain waiting to be discovered. Such was the song of the beauty of a nebulae.

The song of the nebulae wasn't so much a song as it was a rhapsody. It moved in and out of themes and rhythms and melodies like swirling whirlpools of sound. The sheer size and complexity of the music could easily have overwhelmed the diminutive singer, but Gloria rode every wave and movement with effortless ease, taking the lead for much of the piece, with the Dawn Star's voice serving only as support.

The glory of the One grew in brightness as it reflected what the nebulae's song was describing, giving hint to the beauty and majesty of that which had yet to be created. For now, all the wonder and beauty of creation was contained in the songs of the tree. Just as the Dawn Star was the first of the host, the music in the tree of songs was among the first of creation.

When the last notes of the song were given voice, the entire chamber was still and quiet. The eyes of every angel gathered in the tree were fixed toward where Gloria stood. After a moment, she inhaled, sighed, and said simply, "Fun." The entire company gathered in the tree, including the One, burst into applause and laughter.

Soon after the applause ceased, the host began to break off and chatter with one another. Some sang the songs they had already been taught to each other, and some just listened and took it all in. Gloria went from one small group to another, joining in on the conversation when she could, singing with them, or just sitting and observing in quiet contemplation.

"How will she help me?" the Dawn Star asked the One.

"That is for you to determine." The One swept His arm across and over Himself. "There are many songs yet to learn, and you have a vast host of singers waiting to sing them."

The Dawn Star looked around, and as he followed the sweep of the One's hand, he smiled at the thought of his host singing the songs in the tree.

"Gloria is able to hold the songs and teach them to the rest of the host," the One said.

The Dawn Star cocked his head in a silent question.

"She will only teach the songs you pick for her. Some songs will require the voices of many."

The Dawn Star gazed up at Gloria, who sat quietly listening to Allegro and another singing a duet version of the song of the butterfly. She would be his helper, the One had said, because she could hold the songs just like him. He did not know entirely what this new revelation meant, but for now he would receive her as a gift to him from the One, which she was.

13

IN THE CITY

The Dawn Star and Gloria quickly fell into a routine of teaching songs to the host in the tree. By the look, size, and color of individual fruit, the Dawn Star was able to identify the songs he had already learned. With Gloria close by, he would pick one and give it to her, and she would in turn choose the angel to whom she would teach it. The process was slow, but it didn't seem to matter. Each song sung in the tree was greeted with delight by all who sang and heard it.

The Dawn Star made his way through every branch of the tree of songs, learning down to the last note every song he inhaled from the fruit. When most of the tree's songs had been learned and distributed to his host, he heard the familiar contralto voice of the Spirit call his name. He looked down through the branches and saw the Spirit gazing up at him from the base of the tree of songs.

He glided down to where the Spirit stood waiting for him. When the Spirit distinguished Herself from the other members of the One, the Dawn Star became aware of an enveloping warmth that seemed to surround her. As the main identifying characteristic of the One collectively was a bright white light, with the Spirit the light of the glory of the One seemed to be refracted into an ever-changing variety of soft color. The Dawn Star was always pleasantly surprised by the mysterious presence of the Spirit.

She greeted the Dawn Star with a warm smile. "Let's walk together," she said as she moved to leave the chamber of the tree of songs.

The Dawn Star looked up at the tree with a questioning look.

"Oh, they'll be all right," the Spirit answered his unspoken question. "They are in good hands with Gloria. Let them play."

With that, he followed the Spirit out into the great hall, where he discovered all the doors surrounding the hall, including his amethyst doors, to be standing wide open.

As he glanced quickly into the room of readiness, he saw that it was empty of any host and the gleaming swords were missing from its walls. It was also clear that Michael was not in there. In contrast to the silent solitude of the room of readiness, the room of God's word was alive with sounds and activity. Drawn to it, the Dawn Star moved to where the emerald doors stood open and peered into the chamber.

Aside from the images from the books swirling about the room, he observed Gabriel's host scattered from ceiling to floor. Some were sitting, some were standing, and some were dancing and moving with the images. He looked up and saw one angel sitting upside down in a corner of the cathedral ceiling, reading a book with an additional large stack of books beside him. He realized that a multitude of the host were similarly occupied, surrounded by their own stack of books.

He walked to the angel sitting at the table closest to him and read the title of the book she was reading: *The Beloved: Clara.* He glanced at the stack beside her and read other similar titles all beginning with

The Beloved but with different names like Avram, Megan, Chang Yi, and M'Bonye.

The Dawn Star asked, "What are they reading?"

"They're learning about their charges, the members of the beloved they will be watching over and caring for during their time in creation. Now the idea of them only exists in the purple firmament above the great hall and these books."

The Dawn Star looked around the room at the host and their individual stacks of books. "The beloved will be many," he observed.

"Yes," replied the Spirit. Then, almost to herself, she smiled and said, "Many to love."

The Dawn Star moved farther into the room of God's word and made his way to stand behind the angel reading about the beloved named Clara. Looking over her shoulder, he was surprised to see the pages that seemed to hold the angel's attention were blank. There was nothing there for him to read.

Just as he was about to inquire from the Spirit why this was so, a noise of laughter caught the Dawn Star's attention. He turned to see the tall slim figure of Gabriel conversing with the Son in the middle of the room. At first glance it appeared as if Gabriel were speaking to another angel just slightly taller than himself, but the ever-present glory of the One revealed that Gabriel's companion was indeed the Son.

It was the laughter of the Son that had caught the Dawn Star's attention. He looked at the Dawn Star from across the room and waved warmly at the sight of him. He smiled back and nodded as the Son and Gabriel returned to their conversation.

To the Dawn Star, the One collectively was always the focus of whatever room or space He occupied. Even the Spirit with Her ever-fluctuating glory of colors was a centerpiece that one could not easily overlook. But the Son, in contrast, seemed to effortlessly blend into the circumstances around Him. His Glory did not spill from Him as much as it was contained within Him.

As He spoke with Gabriel, the Son seemed intensely interested in what the archangel was saying. He asked questions and nodded as if He were learning something new from this creature of glory that He'd had a hand in bringing to life. With one last glance and smile over to the Spirit and the Dawn Star, Gabriel and the Son turned and disappeared behind a large shelf of books.

"I have something to show you," the Spirit said, gently tugging his arm from behind. The Dawn Star took one last look around the room he loved almost as much as his beloved tree of songs and followed Her across the great hall toward and through the open jade doors and out of the palace of all things.

Standing outside on the portico of the palace with the staircase to God's temple directly in front of him, the Dawn Star looked up to see Michael's host stretched out across the golden sky between the palace and the temple. Michael was positioned in front of them, performing precise movements with his arms, legs, head, and body that were matched perfectly by his host, down to the last angel.

Higher above and behind them was the Father overseeing every detail and movement of Michael's host in front of Him. The appearance of the Father apart from the collective of the One was another contrast from the affable, easy nature of the Son and the Spirit's soft, warm refracted glory. Strength and power distinguished the Father from the others. Even from his vantage point, the Dawn Star could see it manifested as He studiously and carefully watched Michael lead his host in a series of the choreographed movements.

Upon completion of what could only be called a dance, the Father clapped His hands and joyfully shouted, "Yes! Again! Do it again!"

Michael responded with a great joyful laugh of his own.

As the Dawn Star watched intently, he felt the Spirit slip something into his hand.

"I took the liberty of picking this for you for this moment," She said.

He looked down to see a glowing light fruit in the palm of his hand. With the Spirit's nonverbal encouragement, the Dawn Star held the fruit to his face, inhaled, and let the song's fragrance fill his senses as well as his mind. Just as he opened his mouth to sing the new song, Michael's host began their dance.

What the Dawn Star sang was less about melody and lyrics and more about tonal sounds and beats, which were matched perfectly to every movement of Michael's host. The Dawn Star rose from the portico until he was at an even level with Michael and his host. He increased his volume, which was matched equally by the angelic company facing him.

As the song continued, it became repetitious, which allowed Michael and his host to join in. At regular rhythmic intervals from time to time, the host would shout out a loud boisterous "Ah!" As the rhythmic song repeated itself, they all joined in, including the Father and the Spirit. They were even joined by the Son and Gabriel, who wandered out onto the portico along with a good number of Gabriel's host, as well of some of the Dawn Star's own, including Gloria, who were drawn out by the sound of the rhythmic commotion occurring outside the walls of the palace of all things.

After a last boisterous "ah," the Spirit tugged the Dawn Star gently at his elbow and spoke into his ear. "Come with me."

Turning to go with Her, he left the joyous chant of angels and the Godhead behind.

The Spirit led the Dawn Star across the portico in front of the palace of all things and to the left, where there was another set of gold steps that seemed to curve around until they flattened out into a walkway paved with pearl, gold, and silver. Along the path, he could see glimpses of structures through the golden mist, which dissipated before them as they traveled.

"What are those that I see in the mist along the path?" the Dawn Star asked.

"They are for the beloved," the Spirit answered. "All that they achieve and accomplish will be recorded and stored in these buildings for all to enjoy."

The Dawn Star could not fully comprehend what he was being told by the Spirit regarding the beloved, whose concept and identity remained a mystery to him, but the mention of them sparked a question that he gave voice to as they walked along the lane.

"My Lord Spirit, in the room of God's word, one of Gabriel's host was reading a book called *The Beloved: Clara*, yet when I chanced a glimpse at the open pages, they were blank. There was nothing there for me to read. But the angel was looking intently at it as if something were on the page."

"That was Balla who was reading the book, and for her the pages were not blank. In it was written all she will need to know about the beloved who will be called Clara. Along with the One, Balla will be Clara's guardian throughout her life until she is joined with us in heaven."

Confused, the Dawn Star asked, "But why were the pages blank to me?"

The Spirit stopped and faced him. "Because Balla will be Clara's responsibility, not yours. Balla will know everything there is to know about caring for the beloved Clara when it is her time. She will know Clara's mind and heart, her strengths and weaknesses, her gifts and talents, her likes and dislikes. Everything about Clara, down to the last detail, is written in the book that Balla was studying. Only the Father, the Son, and the Spirit know more about Clara than Balla ever will."

"The One," declared the Dawn Star.

"Yes," said the Spirit.

"Because You wrote her book?"

"Yes."

"Will I ever be able to know what is written in Clara's book?" the Dawn Star asked pensively.

"If you are invited to know her," said the Spirit.

"Why would I not be able to know this beloved called Clara?" he asked, taken aback by the Spirit's response.

"Being invited to know someone is a gift a person gives to another. You and your brother angels were brought into the knowledge of the One. It is a gift We gave you because, as the One, We want you to know Us just as you are fully known to the One. It will eventually be the beloved's choice to let themselves be known. It is their gift to give away or withhold. Their gift and no one else's. They will choose."

The Dawn Star said, "The beloved Clara is not yet, but Balla has been given the right to know her. Is she taking something from Clara that has not been given?"

"Balla has been given all the information she needs to serve as Clara's guardian throughout her life according to the will of the One. Gabriel is the steward of the books of the beloved. It is he who selects the guardian for each individual person."

"Is Gabriel able to read what is written in the books of the beloved?" asked the Dawn Star.

"Yes, of course," replied the Spirit. "Just as you are able to hold and sing all the songs in the tree of songs while others could not and assign those songs to members of your host as you see fit. Just as you selected the song of the butterfly for Allegro—excellent choice, by the way—Gabriel selects each book of the beloved for his host and assigns it to them."

The Dawn Star recalled when he was in the chamber of the tree of songs with Michael and Gabriel and how they were unable to grasp the glowing fruit. The responsibilities of each archangel and their host was becoming clearer to him.

They continued their journey along the gold and silver path. After a period of quiet, except for the distant chants of Michael's host as they continued to repeat the chant the Dawn Star had taught them, his mind was still on the books he could not read. It filled him with wonder and questions.

"It would seem that Gabriel will know all about the beloved?" the Dawn Star asked.

"Gabriel will only know what he needs to know to help his host serve their charges as well as they can," replied the Spirit.

"Does the room of God's word belong to Gabriel?"

The Spirit laughed and said, "No more than the tree of songs belongs completely to you. Gabriel's responsibility is to select guardians for each of the beloved. As you are the keeper of the songs, Gabriel is the keeper of the books of the beloved. Other than that, all else that has been written by the One is free to all who make their home in the kingdom of heaven."

The Dawn Star smiled as he took in the Spirit's answer. The memories of the wonders of that room with its swirling, dancing images and the infinite number of volumes on every subject imaginable filled him delight and warmth. He recalled the quiet and stillness of the round chamber where the One had first shown him the home of the beloved. Knowing that he had access to all the room had to offer filled his spirit with gladness. As for knowledge of the beloved, he accepted the idea that he would have to wait until he was invited to know them.

They traveled together in silence. The Dawn Star became aware that he was no longer able to hear the rhythmic chants of Michael and his host. They had either stopped their endeavors or he and the Spirit had traveled far enough that their song could no longer reach them.

"We are here," the Spirit announced.

The Dawn Star looked up and saw the golden mist they were walking through disperse to reveal a tall set of closed doors made completely of glass. Etched in the glass were symbols the Dawn Star did not recognize. They were not words or a picture of anything he knew.

The Spirit rose to the top of the doors, looked down at the Dawn Star, and said, "Listen to what I sing."

With that, She turned to the door, extended Her hand, and began to sing in a language he could not understand. As She sang, She touched each of the symbols, which were arranged in sets of horizontal lines that extended across the doors and down from the top. By the end of the song, She was standing back down by the Dawn Star as the doors slowly opened.

Before the doors could fully reveal what was behind them, the Spirit repeated the song and the doors returned to the closed position. The Dawn Star looked on in wonder, curious as to what the doors were concealing.

The Spirit took the Dawn Star by the hand and led him to the top of the doors, where he came face-to-face with the strange arrangement of symbols, signs, and lines.

Pointing to them, She said, "What is inscribed here is the language of music to open and close the doors. Every song can be written in this language. I am giving this song to you."

The Dawn Star looked on in wonder as he took in what the Spirit was saying.

“To me?” he asked.

“To you and no one else. Sing it with me.”

“I don’t know the language in which you sang the song.”

“In the song you will be asking the doors to open or close,” said the Spirit. “Knowing the exact meaning of each word isn’t necessary for you at this time. Simply sing the words as you heard me sing them.”

With that last instruction, the Spirit began to sing. The Dawn Star matched her with every note and every word of the language he did not understand. From the first hearing, the song was deeply embedded in his heart and memory as if it had always been there.

They ended the song once again at the base of doorway as the doors swung freely open, slowly revealing what waited behind them.

“The doors will only open and close for you now. No other of the host will be able to sing the song of the doors. Your voice, and your voice alone, has the power to open or shut them,” the Spirit declared.

The doors now stood wide open, revealing a vast domed amphitheater completely enclosed by heavily framed cathedral windows that continued in a curve up to the apex of the roof.

When the Dawn Star looked up, he could see the golden clouds of God’s kingdom through the arched panes of glass. The floor of the space sloped down in tiered rows until it flattened out into a perfect circle directly under the apex of the domed ceiling. In the center of the floor was a mosaic representation of the tree of songs with various bright jewels representing the light fruit.

“What is this place?” the Dawn Star asked.

“It is the tabernacle of praise, and it is yours.”

“Mine?”

“Here you will prepare all the songs of creation with your host,” the Spirit said. "Every song from the tree will be sung here together with all your host."

The Dawn Star slowly glided down the tiered steps. He landed in the center of the circle and began to walk around it, taking in all that he saw before him. The cathedral was beautiful in its simplicity. As the light of heaven filtered through the glass, it refracted on the surfaces, filling the vast space with dancing color.

"It's beautiful," he said. "And it's mine?"

"Yes, it is," said the Spirit as She joined the Dawn Star in the center of the of the floor.

"We will sing here?"

"You can sing here now if you would like."

The Dawn Star smiled. He slowly rose from the floor and began to sing a doxology. It seemed to express all the emotions he was feeling at this moment. "Praise God from whom all blessings flow …"

As he sang, the words and music became etched on one of the sets of windowpanes that surrounded the cathedral. He was delighted as he watched his hymn appear before him. His voice, amplified by the acoustics, filled the space fully and completely.

In the middle of the piece, the Dawn Star became aware of the Spirit of the One singing with him. Her contralto voice joined his in perfect harmony. He had sung with others, including the One before, but this was a different experience, a more intimate one. Even as he saw Her singing in the circle below, it felt as if he were totally filled with Her. Her harmony came from inside him. The colorful glory of the Spirit filled the tabernacle of praise along with their voices.

When the song was complete, the Dawn Star was still as he listened to the fading echoes of the song until all was still and quiet. As he descended back to the circle where the Spirit was waiting for him, he looked all around.

When he landed, he said to the Spirit, “Thank you.”

If it was for the tabernacle or the intimacy of the song they had just shared that he was expressing his gratitude, the Dawn Star wasn’t quite sure. Perhaps it was for both. In any case, the Spirit simply smiled and nodded.

After a moment, the Spirit took him by the hand and led him to the open glass doors. “Let’s go and meet them.”

“Who?”

“Your host. They are on their way.” She looked at the Dawn Star and smiled. “I took the liberty of calling for them.”

He heard them coming before he saw them. The Dawn Star and the Spirit stood at the threshold of the great glass doors, which stood wide open, revealing all the simple beauty of the tabernacle of praise. He heard the songs from the tree being sung by his host as they walked toward him on the gold, silver, and pearl path, which ended where they stood.

As he listened to their approach, he looked up and caught sight of the holy temple of the One shining high above them but at some distance from where he It seemed that his tabernacle and the temple stood on opposite ends of the city of God. It was indeed God’s holy temple shining high and far off. There was no mistaking its splendor and glory.

He looked with warmth upon the place that marked his beginning. He then closed his eyes and thought of his beloved tree of songs, where he had first discovered the sheer joy of singing the songs that grew there. He opened his eyes and turned to take in the tabernacle of praise, which marked his continuation and purpose in the kingdom of heaven.

The singing of the host, which became louder, got the Dawn Star’s attention. He turned to see them approaching in full, with the tiny figure of Gloria and the mass of Allegro leading the way. The company stopped short of where the Spirit and the Dawn Star stood. Gloria put up small white hand, and the singing faded away. The host crowded around in stacks up and out to get as close a view as possible.

The Dawn Star looked at the Spirit. With a deferring nod and upturned hand, She yielded to the Dawn Star to speak for them.

He returned the nod and said, "Welcome to the tabernacle of praise!"

With that, the host filed into the glass dome, making sounds of awe and wonder. When they had all entered, the Spirit said to the Dawn Star, "I will leave it with you then."

She faded from view, but Her presence was just as real as if She were still standing close by him. He smiled at the realization that the One was never really gone from his presence. He turned and joined his host inside the tabernacle of praise.

Before the beginning, the time in the city of God was filled with preparations and discoveries. Though all the host seemed to have specific responsibilities according to whom they belonged—Michael, Gabriel, or the Dawn Star—they all seemed to have access to most of what the palace of all things and the city of God had to offer. No one was forbidden to enter any door that was open, and many doors remained that way, allowing access to any who happened to wander in.

The Dawn Star often found members of Michael's and Gabriel's host sitting among the branches of the tree of songs along with his own host, chatting and passing their hands through the light fruit and singing together. In turn, his host as well as others were frequent visitors to the room of God's word, exploring the various books, charts, and diagrams contained within. There was much to know and learn in the kingdom of the One, and the entire host of heaven wanted to learn and know it all.

Though the doors of the tabernacle of praise had not closed since the Dawn Star and the Spirit had sung them open, no one came in and out except the Dawn Star and his host. It was if they were in their own private world, and in that world they sang. Their collective voices raised in song filled the crystal dome and spilled out into the atmosphere of the city of God, inadvertently teaching the angelic host the songs of creation. When they sang the songs, words and music would etch itself onto the glass windows in the form of beautiful script. They sang and rehearsed them all over and over. Each host was assigned a harmony to sing as well as specific solos.

They were rehearsing the song of the butterfly in which Allegro had an intricate lyrical solo involving rapid runs up and down the musical scale. When it was complete, the entire host began to applaud Allegro for his accomplishment.

When it died down, the Dawn Star glided down to him and said, "Well done, my friend," and made to embrace him.

In the middle of the embrace, Allegro said to the Dawn Star, "Thank you, my Lord."

The Dawn Star immediately broke the hug and stepped away from Allegro. "Don't call me that," he said.

The tabernacle became silent except for the Dawn Star's voice. Allegro's usual cheerful face flattened out into an emotionless mask as his eyes widened in surprise.

After a moment, the Dawn Star's face softened. He explained gently, "I am Lucifer. I am the Dawn Star. I am not your Lord. Your Lord … my Lord … is the One, the only Lord of the kingdom of heaven … the Lord and creator of all things." He paused and gently touched the side of Allegro's face "Let's never forget that."

Allegro smiled and said, "I'll remember."

"Good!" said the Dawn Star. "Let's all sing it again."

THE WATERS

The waters originated from the glory of God in the center of the temple, just over the raised dais that served as the throne of the One. They began as nothing more than a slight haze or mist that settled from the cloud of glory overtop the dais like tiny liquid diamonds. The droplets seemed to have a life of their own; they reflected the light of the temple and slowly moved together as if they were drawn to one another by some unknown force. They came together as a small single stream of crystal liquid that trickled off the throne of God and onto the floor in the opposite direction of the great doors that served as the entrance and exit of the holy temple.

Opposite the great doors of the temple were three large arched openings like cathedral windows. They took up the whole width of the temple in place of a wall. The stream of water splashed onto the temple floor, made its way to these openings, and divided into three equal streams that flowed toward each of the three windows. Directly outside the archways there was no threshold, only the edge of the temple and the golden mist and clouds below. Out of the windows the three streams flowed in increasing strength down and through the clouds of heaven to their mysterious destination below.

The waters' flow began shortly after Gloria made her way down the golden staircase as the last of the great host. The Dawn Star often stood in one of the great openings and watched the streams flow and fall from the windows, wondering at their purpose and where they seemed to be going in such a rush.

He liked the sound of the waters' flow and the roaring they made as they rushed down and away from the temple. He would hover over the mist and strain to hear the waters' thunder far below.

For a long time, it was just the waters falling from the temple into the golden clouds, until he observed moving out from under the mist a gathering of the waters in a single place like a pool, a pond, a lake, and then a sea. The sea of the waters grew slow and steady, spreading farther and farther out and away from the temple of the One, which was very high above it.

The Dawn Star did not know the purpose of the waters even as they began to flow out from the golden mist. Though the distance between the temple and the gathering of waters was great in height and depth, some light from the temple still reflected off the surface of this sea like shimmering diamonds. He was left to wonder at the mystery of its creation as he watched the light dance upon the dark still waters even as they flowed farther away from the temple's light.

The color and tone of the mysterious sea was a stark contrast to the color and tone of the city of God. Heaven was filled with life, energy, and indescribable color. It was bright and vibrant. The waters, in their slow and deliberate flow out and away, were dark and deep. Nothing moved above or within. It was a contrast between something and nothing, as if the waters themselves were waiting for something to fill them.

The three archangels often placed themselves in the middle of the arches, hovering just above the waterfalls, and speculated on the purpose of the dark deep water that slowly spread and stretched before them like a dark sea.

Gabriel wondered how all this fit into the One's original design. In all the knowledge that was available to him in the room of God's word, he could find no information regarding the waters. Not one word as far as he knew had been written about them. There were volumes of books about rocks and minerals. He could explain the process of photosynthesis in plants, though they had yet to be created, but of that which stretched out before him in inky darkness, he was ignorant. However, he wisely discerned that the mysterious waters must somehow be connected to all that made up the kingdom of the One. This was all that Gabriel knew for certain, and that all would be revealed at the will of the One.

Similarly, the Dawn Star knew no song for the waters. There were a thousand different songs about a thousand different things from a microbe to the cosmos, and he had learned and sung them all. But he could find no tune hidden in the branches of his beloved tree for the waters. Because of this, he felt a disconnect from them. His songs and singing connected the Dawn Star to everything in heaven, to Michael and Gabriel, the holy temple, his host, the city of God, and especially the One. But because there was no tune for the waters, he could only wonder in bewilderment as to why they existed. For a time, he was content to let the sound of the falls be the song of the waters, but he felt no completion with them, just a separation … detachment.

Michael, as he looked upon them, felt only the need to watch over and protect them. Whatever the purpose of the expanding sea before him, even in its nothingness, the waters had a steadfast guardian in the bronze archangel.

The thoughts and musings of the individual archangels regarding the waters were kept to themselves. The only thing they shared with each other was a silent curiosity.

The waters continued to grow and expand, and from the vantage point of the temple, there was more of the dark water visible on the horizon than the golden mist of heaven. Then the horizon disappeared altogether and there was only the inky, dark water that seemed to stretch far beyond the boundaries of heaven. There was no way to discern the end to them, if there was an end at all.

Often the One—who all the city of God knew as the one true God, the Lord, the Creator of heaven and all that lived and dwelled within it—stepped out upon the dark, deep waters and walked in and upon them. While the angels wondered and were curious about them, they did so from the close familiar confines of the holy temple. In contrast, the One ventured out into the growing shadowy sea to stroll among it as if He were walking the lanes and corridors of His own city. Though He traveled far out into the darkness, the darkness never consumed the light of His glory, because there was nothing there to consume it. The One's light was always visible, no matter the distance. He was always the brightest in heaven, and it was true even with the waters.

Though the Dawn Star and the other angels were never forbidden to accompany the One as He took His walks over the waters, they were also never invited and they didn't think to ask. Those moments only belonged to the One, shared by no one else. To insert oneself into those moments would seem like an intrusion.

The One never spoke of the waters. Neither were they ever discussed by the citizens of heaven. The only acknowledgment that they existed at all came from the archangels' curious vigilance and the One's solitary journeys out onto them. It was as if the waters held a secret that no one dare speak of, for to speak of the waters would be to make them something that they were not.

The real truth of the waters was that they were nothing. They were filled with nothing. There were no preconceived expectations or notions regarding them. As nothing, the waters were unblemished, uncluttered, unencumbered with other ideas other than what the One had planned for them. As nothing, they held a promise hidden only in the mind and will of the One.

What no one knew in heaven except for Him was that the waters were the foundation of the beginning. From them would come all things that were to be created. Upon them it would start …

And then … the waters ceased flowing from the temple.

The great falls fell silent.

The three silver streams that came from the throne of God dissipated into the jeweled floor of the temple as if they never were.

All that remained of them was the vast, dark, empty sea of nothing.

The three archangels stood in the cathedral openings of the holy temple and watched as the One stepped out upon the waters and said, “Now it begins.”

15

THE BEGINNING

The entire host of heaven gathered in and around the holy temple to witness what would come next. The three archangels stood in the open cathedral windows, the Dawn Star in the center and Michael and Gabriel to the left and right of him respectively. Gloria sat above them on what could be considered the roof, her tiny legs dangling over the edge. The rest of the host found their observation posts as best they could, stacking themselves in rows going up and out.

Without being told, Michael's host positioned themselves in an orderly fashion, poised and ready for what would come next. They stood silent in their disciplined observation.

The rest of the hosts chatted excitedly to one another in anticipation for this moment. Ever since they were formed into existence, they had all prepared for what was to come. They learned every song and detail of the coming creation. They could describe in detail the physics required for the wind to blow without feeling or seeing the effect it had on the objects with which it came in contact.

Gabriel's host could recall an infinite number of names that the members of the beloved would be called without knowing who and what they were, only that they were called the beloved.

For the Dawn Star, his great purpose would soon come to pass. He and his host would sing the songs of all creation. Before a tree took root, he knew it's song. Before the birds could take flight, he knew the tune they would sing, down to the last note. He knew the purr and deep rumblings of the great cats before they even began to patrol the Earth.

To the host, what was only an idea, a wish, a desire, a dream of what was to be was about to come true. The noise and chatter among the host diminished until they watched in complete silence as the One moved out, above, and over the waters.

The One moved farther away from where the heavenly host was gathered in and around the temple. Though the distance increased, the glory of the Lord never diminished. More to truth, it along with the One seemed to grow in strength and size.

When the One had reached a certain distance that could have been the exact center of whatever the waters were, He stopped. The Dawn Star and the rest of the host observed the three that made up the One become more visible to one another and begin conversing with one another, much like he had witnessed them do at the creation of his brother archangels.

Their conversation was observed and unheard until such time that a sound gradually made its way across the vastness of the waters. It was a song sung as one in three voices. It was no song that had ever been heard before. The language was indiscernible to the Dawn Star, strange and ancient, reminding him of when he had stood by the One before the amethyst doors as He sang them open to reveal the tree of songs.

The tune that came across the waters was a more haunting melody that grew in size and complexity as the song went on. The Dawn Star felt as if it were a song for the moment, for that which was and would never be again. Everything would change for the better, he had no doubt, but it will be different now.

In his mind, he thought of when it was just he and the One, before his brothers, before Gloria and the rest of the host. He was grateful for the intimacy of that "only time" with the One. He looked to his right and to his left at Gabriel and Michael and smiled at the thought of the three of them together and the feeling of being more complete with them. The joy of the "only time" was shared with them and eventually the entire host of heaven. If nothing else were to happen, the Dawn Star felt satisfied and content with how things were, content and complete with just the city of God and heaven only … nothing else.

But he knew something else was coming as the song from across the waters washed over them. They had all been preparing for it, singing and learning about it.

At the center of the preparation was the idea of the beloved. All was for the sake of the beloved, whoever or whatever that was. The time of the beloved was coming, and the song of the One was marking that time as now.

Then the song ended.

The One stood still over the face of the waters in silence. No one moved. The silence engulfed them all. Every mind was still as they waited for what would come next. The stillness was so pervasive that it seemed to have its own strength and identity. If any sound attempted to make itself heard, it was most likely swallowed up by the stillness before it reached any ear to acknowledge its existence.

Then the One spoke, and the silence was broken …

"Let there be light!"

As He spoke, the One lifted his head and stretched His arms out wide. This was something the Dawn Star had never seen before. It looked as if the One were in complete surrender to what would come next … a total commitment to what would be His creation.

As the word was spoken, a speck of light rose out of the open mouth of the One, almost lost amid the glory of God but still making itself known and seen as it rose above the One, shining above Him like a single star. As it rose higher, it grew in size until it was almost the height and breadth of God and His glory.

At a certain distance, it stood still and rested above the One. As it kept its place, the Dawn Star and the host observed the light change in color and properties. It was becoming more than just a single light, but many lights swirling amid clouds and vapors in choreographed circular movements that increased in speed and intensity … until the One laughed.

The Dawn Star remembered in the room of readiness when the One laughed and the hall lit up with light and color that spread across the ceiling. In this case, the sound of God's laughter hit the great light above Him like a physical thing, causing it to suddenly explode.

Upon impact with God's laugh, the light burst out from the One in every direction—above and below, left and right, and front and back. For a moment, the great burst and the One could not be distinguished from each other. The dark water disappeared, and there was only light. It dazzled the eyes of the host of witnesses observing from the holy temple. The blast brought with it great warmth and euphoric joy that washed over all of them. It was nothing any of them had experienced before.

And then it was gone, leaving only the glory of the One as if nothing had happened, but the memory of the warmth and joy the light had brought remained. But something had changed. The dark nothingness of the waters was replaced by a firmament of a deep, velvety blue-black.

The One kept still for a long time, while the host began to stir, asking questions of one another about what would come next. The Dawn Star watched the One in silence as He began to make the long journey back toward the holy temple.

"What just happened?" Michael asked. "God spoke the light into existence, and now it's gone."

"I don't think so," mused the Dawn Star.

"Wait for it," Gabriel said.

"What?" said Michael. "What are we waiting for?"

Gabriel stood still and quiet as he looked out over the dark blue firmament … searching. Then he quietly said, "There it is!" He pointed at a tiny single light as it winked in the darkness just over the shoulder of the One, who continued to move toward them.

The Dawn Star had actually heard it before it winked in. It was a faint sound in his mind similar to what happened when he inhaled the light fruit from the tree of songs. He heard the tune and saw the lyrics. It was the song of light. It must have come to him when the burst of light washed over them. As more and more tiny lights appeared in the dark, the song of light began to make its way to the Dawn Star's lips in the form of a simple hum.

"How did you know?" Michael asked Gabriel.

"The One must have dispersed the light to the farthest boundaries of the waters. It is making its way back to us over the great distance. What we see now is the light that is closest to us."

Michael and the Dawn Star both looked at Gabriel in wonder.

He simply said, "I read about it in *Light and Its Properties: Volume 1*."

At this, the hummed tune on the Dawn Star's lips turned into a song sung aloud as more and more lights blinked into view. It was quickly picked up by the rest of his host, with Gloria leading the way. As the One completed His journey back to the temple, the entire host of heaven sang the song of light. The One turned and looked out upon the dark water, which was now filled with a multitude of lights that continued to twinkle, blink, and wink into place.

The One joined his voice to the song being sung by His host, and as He sang, the warmth and joy that was felt by the burst of light returned upon the host in full force. They sang the song over and over with different parts and nuances added to each run through.

The Dawn Star stepped out of the arch in which he stood and began to sing even louder. Putting himself between the temple and the One, he rose into the air, completely lost in the moment.

When the song ended in a loud harmonic crescendo, more of the bright lights had come into view. Some of the lights seemed very close, yet others remained small and tiny, brought on by the great distance they inhabited.

The great nothing of the dark water was gone. A newly created universe had taken its place. Lights continued to appear as the One slowly looked around at what He had just made, His host, the archangels, and finally the Dawn Star.

Then He declared to all at which He was looking, "The dark you see is now the night, and the light is the day! The first day!" Then the One declared, "This is good!"

A PLACE FOR LIFE

When the One stepped again into what was once just the waters, more of the specks of light had appeared and a large mass of light spiraled at a great distance away at the exact center of their view. It reminded the Dawn Star of what he had seen when the One opened the scroll in the quiet round chamber inside the room of God's word. What they saw before them was exactly like what had emerged from the scroll when it was unrolled. The Dawn Star remembered what the One had called it—a galaxy—and the One was walking directly toward it.

There were many such galaxies of varying shapes and sizes filling the dark firmament, but it was the one in the center that God seemed most interested in. As the One moved closer to the galaxy, it seemed to move closer to Him and those observing from the holy temple. It was as if they were all being drawn into its center, deeper and farther. They were about two-thirds of the way from the bright center of the newly formed galaxy when the One stopped along an outer spiral arm.

The One came to a bright gaseous patch of light that had no form to speak of. It was more spindly tendrils of white flame and particles moving in opposite directions than anything else. It was constantly changing in shape and size like some wild, uncontrolled thing. In its out-of-control state, bits of surrounding gas and objects in space were quickly drawn to it and just as quickly cast away from it.

The Dawn Star and the rest of the host observed the One move slowly to it with arms spread. The palms of His hands faced toward the seemingly out-of-control patch of light. The voice of the One could be heard speaking in gentle, calming tones.

"Shh. Settle down … So much power. You need something to do with all that power … something to watch over."

Upon those words, a small group of lights emerged from the mouth of the One, nine in all. He took each of the nine lights in hand and seemed to speak to them individually, though the Dawn Star and the host could not hear what was being said. After each "conversation," the tiny specks of light quickly moved to a specific destination away from the patch of light and gas, as if responding to orders, which they were indeed doing.

As each speck of light took up its assigned station, it began to orbit around the One and the patch of light and, at the same time, take on its own specific character. When the lights had settled into their specific routes and speeds around the patch of light, the One looked to His host observing from the temple and declared with a gesture, "These will be called planets."

The nine planets were of varying sizes and shapes, from the tiny farthest planet to the four gaseous giants that preceded inward. As these continued to grow and change in hues of blue, pale green, gold, brown, and red, they drew into themselves from the surrounding space bits of material that developed into rings that encircled them or became complete separate objects of the individual planets' systems.

As the planets and their individual systems came into their own character, the Dawn Star noticed it was as if they were also coming into obedience to the patch of light they all circled. They were now under its control. The patch of light itself seemed to also settle into what it was supposed to be, as if it, too, seemed to respond in obedience to the will of the One.

The four planets closest to the patch of light also became obedient to the small star whose power and authority they were all now under.

As the Dawn Star observed the growth and development of what would come to be known as the solar system, he became aware of a prevailing order that was being established in this great space as each body fell into an assigned sense of obedience to the others. Each of the planets' smaller satellites obeyed the will of their planetary host, even as the planets themselves seemed to obey the will and power of the star at their center, never altering or straying away from that which held them there. The once wild and uncontrollable patch of light seemed to settle into a quiet, unspoken obedience to the will and desires of the One.

The reason for this obedience was not known by the Dawn Star. He suspected Gabriel couldn't provide a sufficient answer either, even with all the books he'd read in the room of God's word, to explain why this was so. It just was the natural way of all created things to obey the will of the One, and the result of that obedience was perfect order.

After He established the planets, the One positioned Himself a third of the way from the new star and its family of satellites. The glory of His presence almost filled the entire space between the second and fourth planet. The One let Himself be taken around by the orbit of the sun several times. Each time around, the glory of God seemed to adjust in speed until it settled on one that seemed to suit the One. The Dawn Star and the rest of the host observed the One orbit the star over and over. At the same time, the other planets settled even more into their own appointed paths.

Whatever would happen next, the One seemed to be in no hurry to accomplish it. To the Dawn Star, He looked to be enjoying exactly where he was in the company of the newly formed solar system, taking in the unique beauty of each planet.

"They're going to enjoy all of this," the One said, whether to Himself or to the host, the Dawn Star wasn't sure.

The host watched the One continue to slowly orbit the sun between the second and fourth planet, all the while leaving a bright trail of glory to completely encircle the star.

As the host of heaven looked on, a new song made its way across the vast distance between themselves and the One. As it was on the first day when God created light, this song was sung in a language known only to the Three who made up the One. The tune was bright, which invoked feelings of hope and joy. It was sung in a bouncy rhythm. While the song sung before the creation of light had invoked a nostalgic feeling of what was, this new song celebrated the promise and idea of what would be.

At the end of the song, the One spoke. "I want there be a place for life!"

As He spoke, another of the tiny specks of light that circled the heart of God made its way to the mouth of the One. He gently caught it in the palm of His hand and held it there, gazing at it lovingly, for quite some time.

The One turned His attention to a small dark ball beside him. It had gone unnoticed by the rest of the host because of its size and lack of distinguishing color. The colorless planet seemed to blend in with the darkness of the universe surrounding it. Were it not for the One's intense interest, it would have continued to orbit the sun, virtually ignored by the rest of the universe and heaven.

The One, still holding the speck of light, placed His hands around the dark planet. As He did so, the light in the One's hand dispersed itself evenly around the surface of the ball. As the light came upon the planet, the host was drawn closer to it in such a way that the other planets, the galaxy, and the stars disappeared from view and this solitary gleaming body was all they could see before them.

The One appeared in the middle the light, and the Dawn Star and the rest of the host observed Him inhale deeply. As He did so, the light of the planet seemed to diminish by half as if the One were taking it into Himself.

After breathing it in, the One held it there for quite some time. All were silent, waiting for what would come next. The One, with His eyes closed, smiled to Himself in secret delight, enjoying the moment of what would come next in this moment of creation. The One then lifted His head and exhaled.

This was not the first time the Dawn Star had observed the power of the breath of God. He remembered the One literally breathing the host into existence. Now as He slowly exhaled, that which was once colorless light changed to a shade of blue unseen before. It started just above the head of the One until it completely surrounded and encased the once-dark planet. The indication that this part of creation was complete was indicated by a soft breeze felt by the Dawn Star on his face, through his hair, and in his wings. He closed his eyes and breathed in a new sensation—the simple joy of breathing in clean, fresh, newly created air from a bright blue atmosphere.

When the Dawn Star opened his eyes, he discovered that the new world had changed. There was the blue firmament above them, and below it were waters. Not the dark, still, empty waters of before, but a sea reflecting the azure blue above it, which rippled with the effect of a gentle breeze blowing over them.

"A zephyr," the Dawn Star said with a smile to himself as the song of that warm, gentle breeze formed upon his lips. As he sang, he was joined by a small group of his host, which included Gloria and Allegro.

It was the song that made clear the true identity of what a zephyr really was. Up until then, it was only a set of figures and directions written on a chart rolled up in a cabinet in the room of God's word. Now it was real. It was all real; the light, the galaxies, the planets revolving around the once-wild, untamed sun, and this the waters under the blue firmament were all coming to pass. They were no longer ideas and images found in a book. They were all here now, right in front of them, with much more to come.

The One pointed above Him and declared, "Sky!" He continued as He swept His arms above Him. "It will protect this place from the harshness of what lies beyond it."

The Dawn Star had no concept of harshness or the word *protect.* Michael, however, who was next to him, nodded in silent affirmation as if he understood the full meaning of the One's words and what they implied.

Some of the host looked and repeated what God had declared the blue firmament to be: "Sky."

Another song surfaced in the Dawn Star's memory. When he had first learned the song from the light fruit, he had only a vague understanding of the blue in his memory. Now it was before him in all its truth and glory.

As the Dawn Star sang the sky song, the presence of the One began to circle the blue planet. As He moved from one place to other, glimpses of what was above the blue firmament could be seen peeking through.

When the One returned to the place where He had begun, He said, "We have had an evening and a morning. Another day is complete!"

Then the One looked above and all around at what He had just created and declared, "This, too, is good. So good."

FROM OUT OF THE SEA

The host of heaven congregated at the holy temple as they watched the One move between the sky and the blue sea until He stopped a great distance from them. From the temple, the Dawn Star, his brother archangels, and the host observed all the works of creation. It was the only place in the city of God that they could watch the Lord do the work of creation.

As before, they observed a small light make its way from the heart of God to the mouth of the One, and like before, He held it in His hand for a long while and smiled. What He was thinking was a mystery to those who watched from their vantage point at the holy temple.

Then the One declared, "Let there be a solid foundation!"

With that, the Dawn Star watched as the Lord slowly sank into the water. The light of the One remained above the surface of the sea for a long time until it, too, was completely immersed.

Beneath the water, the glory of God shone brightly, changing the color of the sea into a bright shimmering gold. The glory of the Lord remained submerged for a long time. The Dawn Star and the rest of the host became aware of a stillness that had settled around them. They were barely aware of each other's presence, though they were all crowded together in and around the temple. The stillness was visibly noticeable upon the waters; once the glory of the One slipped beneath the surface, the water became as glass. There was no movement whatsoever above or beneath, just the glory of God shining through the still waters, as the Dawn Star and the rest of the host waited for what would come next.

Without warning, the surface of the sea directly above the glory of God began to roil and splash violently. The action created great waves across the entire expanse of the sea.

Shortly after the sea came to sudden life, the glory of the Lord began to break through the surface, and in the midst of the emerging glory was the figure of the One rising toward the sky, standing on something that was only a glimpse of what would be, as portrayed in the books written by the hand of God. The One was bringing up what would be declared as dry land from the depths of the sea.

At first it was just the one peak the Lord was standing on. Then more land emerged from the waters. As steep crags and rock-covered mountains revealed themselves, the sea expressed its joy with great waves that exploded into white fireworks of foam as the land crashed itself against them. The water was so active, it was as if the entire sea were applauding the new arrivals into creation.

As this drama unfolded before the host, the Dawn Star thought of the songs in the tree and of one he had taught to an angel called Adagio. Looking around among the host, he caught the eye of Adagio, who was already looking knowingly at him. With a nod from the Dawn Star, he began to sing.

The song began as not so much a tune but rather a low rumble of sounds that came from the lowest register of bass notes. They were a vocal match to the rumblings of the land coming into being. As Adagio sang, he was joined by a chorus of voices in bass, baritone, and tenor. From the initial rumblings, a slow melodic tune emerged in increasing strength. It was an anthem unlike any heard or sung so far. It contained within it the very character and power the new world would possess and indeed already did.

The anthem of the land continued as more peaks emerged and formed valleys, capturing some of the water between them. Where the world was once just sky and sea, it was now being divided and separated by tall summits and rolling hills.

As he watched the land, sky, and sea come together as one, the Dawn Star thought of all the individual things that had a separate beauty in themselves and existing in contentment alone without others, much like the time when it was just he and the One. It could have remained that way, but when Michael and Gabriel had come into being, he had known a completeness like never before. As he looked around for his brother archangels, it seemed as if the three of them were living embodiments of the drama taking place before them. He, the Dawn Star, was like the sky and the air, making the songs he sang a part of the atmosphere around them. Gabriel was the sea, flowing and adapting according to the knowledge of God's word. And Michael was like that which was rising from the water in even more abundance, strong, powerful, and solid yet filled with a great joy.

When the land and rocky crags had finished rising from the sea, the One stepped down from the peak upon which He stood and came to the holy temple, where His host awaited Him.

When the Lord came to them, He turned around and exclaimed, "Wow! Look at that!" He spoke as if it all had taken Him by surprise.

All the host of heaven saw how God had raised the land from the sea and how it covered almost a third of what was once just water. But now, upon the Lord's suggestion, it was like they were seeing it all for the first time: great peaks descending into rolling hills and eventually flat vast tablelands, along with endless varieties of land formations, including steep valleys. They watched in awe as the sea, which had become streams and rivers, cut into the land to form canyons in graduating layers of color.

The Dawn Star looked at the dancing eyes of the One as He looked upon that which He had just made. What he saw in them could be best described in one word: delight. The Lord was delighted.

For a long time, all of heaven, along with the One, took it all in, seeing the whole world at once, as well as every detail. Gabriel was particularly interested in how the water reacted to the land. It was as if God were using the water like a sculpture's tool, slowly chipping and wearing away at the land, creating an ever-changing beauty.

The Dawn Star enjoyed and appreciated the different ways the land masses seemed to frame the sky above and, in contrast, how the flat lands and the sky seemed to become as one. He marveled at how the land and the sea shared the same level of space but the sky shared its domain with nothing else, as if God had appointed it to be the ruler of all that was beneath it.

Michael was occupied with the land itself, looking for and finding in the example of minerals and elements reminders of what was already in the city of God.

"Look there!" he said as he nudged at the Dawn Star and pointed to a yellow vein of material entwining its way through a formation of stone. "That looks just like you!"

The Dawn Star smiled and nodded in agreement.

The One spoke again. "Now there is dry land to go with the sea." With one hand, He indicated the land, and with the other, the One indicated the water. “The earth and the sea. This, too, is good. So good.”

After a long pause, the One continued. “ … But there’s more.” He smiled. “I want the world to be filled with green, lots and lots of green.” With that, another speck of light emerged from the heart of God and came to rest on His outstretched hand.

Within but a moment of it resting there, the One quickly flung it out away from Him. Just as quickly, another took its place and was tossed away like the first. This drama repeated itself, and the specks of light were scattered until all the land was touched by them. When the lights landed, they seemed to melt into the earth until patches of pale green were the only indication they had even been there at all.

The host watched as some of the pale green patches deepened in color and spread in size. As this was happening, the Dawn Star heard the distinctive contralto voice of the Spirit say to him, “Sing all the songs of the plants and trees.”

Immediately all the songs that pertained to the Spirit’s request burst upon his mind, almost to the point of being overwhelming. But without letting a moment pass, he opened his mouth and sang.

He sang the songs of grass in the fields, trees heavy with fruit, splendorous trees that grew straight and tall … and much more. He was aided by his host, who all joined him in singing the songs of green that they were assigned.

The voices of the Dawn Star’s host filled all of heaven and the Earth as well. As they sang, what they were singing about grew before them. The grass in the fields carpeted the great flat plains. Heather and gorse grew on the moors of the Earth. Trees with giant limbs stretching out away from their trunks became forests that covered much of the land. There were shrubs and bushes, and plants and trees with great broad leaves. There was vegetation for almost every part of the world, and a song that was sung for everything that grew.

The Dawn Star and his host continued to sing until all the land was covered in green.

The One said, "That's good," and all the songs of the plants and the trees came to a clean perfect ending.

Then God looked at His heavenly host and said, "Come, look, and see. Walk around, enjoy them … have fun."

For the first time since the work of creation began, the Dawn Star, his brothers, and all their hosts left the confines of the holy temple and began to walk around and all through the new world that God had created. There was an evening and a morning. The third day was complete … and it was good.

18

THE SUN, MOON, AND STARS

The host of heaven traveled the entire length of the land, exploring the mountains, forests, fields, and meadows. They climbed trees and leaped from tall peaks. They raced each other along the plains. They hid from one another in the jungles and took turns finding each other.

In heaven, they were occupied with various responsibilities that came with being a part of a particular host. They learned and sang songs together, they studied books of the beloved, and they learned to work together as one. Every angel agreed that what they did and the duties they carried out in the city of God brought them great joy.

But what they were doing now was different. They were experiencing joy for the sake of joy itself. They were playing. It seemed that the only reason all the angels of heaven were given access into the new creation was for the purpose of having fun.

The Dawn Star, Michael, and Gabriel sat together on a rocky promontory with ocean waves crashing below and the bows of a large tree stretching wide above. They sat in silence for a long time while their various hosts occupied themselves with the wonders of the new world.

Gabriel broke the silence. “What do you like best so far?”

Michael and the Dawn Star looked at one another, not really understanding the question.

“In this place …” His hand swept around to indicate their surroundings. “Of all of this, what is your favorite?”

The Dawn Star shrugged and said, “I like all of it.”

Michael nodded in agreement.

“What’s your favorite?” the Dawn Star asked.

Gabriel stood and said, “I’ll show you.”

With that, he leaped from the edge of the cliff and dove straight into the ocean. Just as quickly, he shot up through the surface with water trailing behind him. When he arrived at the same level as the Dawn Star and Michael, they saw that his hands were cupped as if trying to conceal something.

“This is my favorite!” he said as he tossed the water he had brought up with him into the surprised faces of his two brothers and flapped his wet wings in their direction, drenching them further, all the while laughing like he had never laughed before.

The Dawn Star and Michael stood up, shaking the sea water from themselves and giving each other a nod. They jumped simultaneously from the cliff and tackled Gabriel in midair, accompanied by jovial shouts and laughter. The trio wrestled together until they plummeted into the sea as one large angelic ball. Emerging from the water, they continued to jostle and cavort among the waves. At one point, Michael rose into the air, grabbing Gabriel’s arms as he ascended out of the water. At the last minute, the Dawn Star latched onto Gabriel’s feet and pulled against Michael’s upward motion. It was as if they were in some great tug-of-war with their brother archangel as the rope.

Just when it seemed the Dawn Star would prevail in returning them back to the sea, Michael, with a great thrust of his wings, lifted farther into the sky, taking both his brothers with him. At a certain altitude, Michael began to swing Gabriel, with the Dawn Star still holding onto his feet, in front of him and then behind him, the arc increasing in size with every pass.

At one point when the two of them were swinging out and away from Michael, the Dawn Star chose to let go of Gabriel's feet and allowed the momentum of the swing to propel him farther into the air, accompanied by several somersaults and a great shout As the Dawn Star flew higher and farther away, Michael and Gabriel returned to the rocky promontory and watched their brother until he disappeared from view altogether.

As the Dawn Star flew, he twisted and rolled to take in the vistas that lay above and below him, the deep blue of the sky and the great patches of green that were scattered around the globe, and water with slashes of white caused by the wind rushing over it. *This is it*, he thought. *This is my favorite.*

If it was just the flying or the wind lifting him higher without effort or the ability to take in God's new creation in one view, the Dawn Star wasn't sure. Perhaps it was all of it. Being in the air alone yet not lonely felt masterful to him. He was always mindful of the One and the joy that always permeated his thoughts of Him. But flying through the air unencumbered by anything or anyone was a different kind of joy. He felt like he could do anything he wanted in the air. He was free, as if he were bending the very air to his own personal will. That was it. It was the air itself that was his favorite. It now was his favorite place to be, and it was all his. It was a strange and foreign yet exhilarating feeling to be at this moment independent from anything and anyone.

The voice of the One shook him out of his personal revelry: "Come to the large savanna!"

Evidently it was a command for the entire host, because as he made his way to the place on the land to which he had been called, he saw all the host of heaven traveling to the same location along with his brother archangels.

The One stood in the middle of a great flat land as the host in their three groups gathered around Him. The Dawn Star alighted on the ground to join his host at the front. As if according to a silent command, all the voices on the plain became still and quiet.

The One said. "Today is a new day! There will be lights in the sky to be seen in the day and in the night. They will be for the beloved signs of seasons and the days and the years."

Up to this point, the light that had shined upon the new world had been generated completely and solely by the glory of God and that which came from it. The plants, the trees, the forests, and the grasses were nourished to life by the light of the One.

When He spoke again, the Dawn Star was not sure who He was addressing: "It's your time to shine now, little one."

With that word, the glory of God began to peel away from the sky and return to the One, revealing a dark indigo sky. For a moment, the observing host was in complete darkness. Soon shades of deep pinks and orange appeared just above the eastern horizon. The new colors gradually spread up and brightened that which was once indigo, turning it to lighter shades of blue. It became brighter and brighter until a hint of white-yellow light could be observed peeking over the horizon.

"Ah, there you are," said the One to Himself, smiling.

This rising light was reflected on all the faces of the heavenly host, who stood transfixed as it rose and transformed the world from darkness into light.

"It's the sun," Gabriel said quietly.

The One could be heard chuckling softly in affirmation of Gabriel's declaration.

Indeed, the wild patch of light from before was now making its way up and over the edge of the Earth, brightening the sky as it went and bringing a gradual warmth upon all those who observed its progress. The Dawn Star closed his eyes and smiled as the rising sun bathed his face in warmth and light.

One of the host observed, "It moves so slowly."

Gabriel said, "The sun is not moving at all … well, at least not in the way one would think. The Earth is moving around itself, very slowly allowing the sun, which is fixed in its place, to shine on different parts of the land in different ways."

Whether or not Gabriel's answer was sufficient for the questioner was not fully known, but it would do for a time as the One and his host followed the journey of the sun across the sky.

With the constant light of God's glory upon the Earth, everything had looked the same way. The colors of the rocks, plants, and trees had stayed the same. Now with the sun, the colors of the earth and sea were in almost constant flux depending on how the sun's light affected them. The color of leaves changed between various shades of green, from dark to pale and back, depending on where the sun was in the sky.

The most noticeable difference of the sun's effect on the earth was the shadows produced by individual objects when the light hit them from a particular angle. The part of the object that was not exposed to the sunlight was in a darkness. The shadows created by the phenomena were new creations in and of themselves, lending a whole new dynamic to the beauty of what was already created.

"This light," said the One, pointing to the sun, "will be the steward of the day and watch over it. The sun will bring all life to all the earth and sustain it. All the years of the beloved will be measured and nurtured by it."

It was then that the Dawn Star recalled a song, a hymn he learned at the tree of songs, which he in turn had taught to his host in the tabernacle of praise. After the Dawn Star sang the opening line, his host joined in together to continue the hymn of the rising sun.

As dictated by the hymn as it was learned, the voices of the Dawn Star's host divided into several harmonic parts even beyond the conventional division between low and high voices. At some, point the separate harmonies and counterpoints were too numerous to count. But with all its melodic intricacies, it seemed as if it were being sung by one great voice.

The hymn of the rising sun spoke of its glory and power over the Earth but reminded the listener before its conclusion that there was no glory greater than the One's, the glory of the Lord of hosts. When it ended with a rising crescendo of voices, the last note could be a heard echoing across the great savanna long after the hymn had ended. The Earth to this point had never heard a song so majestic as had just been sung by the entire host of the one called the Dawn Star.

As the host on the plain watched the sun slowly arc across the sky, the Dawn Star pondered the words of the One, especially regarding the beloved. It seemed that even the sun, with all its raw power, would be put into service to the beloved, who or whatever the beloved would be. He found himself smiling in a quiet excitement in anticipation of the beloved's long-awaited appearance.

When the sun began to descend back toward the western horizon, the shadows grew longer and deeper. The sky began to change color from blue, pale orange to brilliant pinks and violets as the sun slowly disappeared below the horizon.

The Dawn Star, along with rest of the host, noticed that as the sun sank, the stars in the universe could be observed through the vail of the sky. When the light of sun was completely gone, the dark inky sky was filled with stars too numerous to count. The blanket of stars covered the entire length and breadth of the sky from north to south and east to west.

The One looked up, swept His arms across the night sky, and declared, "All of these shall keep watch over the Earth and all that dwell within it through the dark of the night. They shall guide the path of the beloved even at night whether on land or sea. They will be a source of great wonder for them."

The Dawn Star was curious as to this declaration. The One indicated that the beloved would be something that would have the entire Earth as their domain. The different varieties of green life seemed to be designated to specific regions of the world, from mountains and plains to jungles and forests. But it seemed the paths of the beloved would take them wherever they desired to go with no boundaries to restrict them.

What extraordinary creatures these beloved will be to have the whole world at their disposal, the Dawn Star thought.

Shortly after the Lord's declaration regarding the stars, a pale ghostly light began to appear on the eastern horizon. It came in the same manner as the sun, slowly, but its light was considerably less powerful and not as influential upon the land as its daytime relative.

Where the sun's shape and size could barely be discerned because of its bright, blinding power and light, that which now came over the horizon was gentler in its power and demeanor. It seemed to glow as opposed to shine. It revealed its shape as a perfectly round sphere, predominantly white with patches of gray in various shades dotting its surface. Some of the stars dimmed from view as it crossed the sky.

"What is that?" Michael asked within the hearing of his brothers.

"It is called the moon. It is the Earth's constant companion around the sun, as it orbits the Earth," Gabriel said in a matter-of-fact manner.

The Dawn Star and Michael were looking at Gabriel when Michael said, "I have to read more."

His brothers chuckled at his response.

When the new object reached its zenith in the night sky and all the host were bathed in its soft, pale light, the One spoke again. "This lesser light shall rule the night. It will measure the months and be a sign for the seasons for the beloved. It will watch over them as they rest."

Again, something for the beloved, thought the Dawn Star.

From the midst of the host, another song made its way through the company on the plain. The soft, melodic tune spoke of the comforting light of the stars and the moon. The Dawn Star immediately recognized the song and the singer because he had personally given the lullaby of the night sky to Gloria to sing. As it went on, several other voices joined in, including the Dawn Star.

The new song was sung as the moon continued its path toward the western horizon, until it disappeared and the stars alone were left to rule the night in its place.

The One walked toward the Dawn Star and said to him, "It will soon be morning. Walk with me. I want to show you something."

He began to walk away from the great host on the plain, and the Dawn Star followed. They were walking side by side at some distance from the rest of the company when he said to the Lord, "This is all so wonderful … You are wonderful. I continue to marvel at all that is being prepared here for the beloved." The Dawn Star swept his arms across the starry sky and continued. "Oh, what they must be to have all of this given to them."

The One smiled knowingly at him in silence as if to say, *"If you only knew."* He pointed to the eastern horizon and said, "Look there!"

The Dawn Star looked to where the One pointed. Just as the sky was turning a pale lavender, he observed a small singular white dot set apart from the other stars, not far above the horizon line.

"That's yours," said the One.

"That star?" he asked.

"Yes," the One replied. "Actually, it isn't a star. It's a planet reflecting the light of the star shining on it. Among other things, it will be called the Dawn Star."

"That's me!" he said with surprised delight.

"Yes," the One replied. "The sun's light reflects on that planet …"

Finishing the thought, the Dawn Star said, "… just like You reflect on me."

"Exactly," said the One. "You were the first, the bringer of songs, the bringer of light and inspiration. You are the first joy of the morning. The beloved will look upon your star and know that the night has passed and the new day is coming with joy and promise. You are a reflector of my glory."

They were silent for a moment as the night sky paled and faded and the light of the new morning took its place. When his star could no longer be seen above the brightening horizon, the Dawn Star said quietly, "Thank you," and the One's only reply was a smile.

As they walked back toward the gathering on the plain, the Dawn Star thought of all the planets that orbited the sun and asked, "Which planet is it?"

"One that is not far from the sun," the One said.

The Dawn Star thought, *Just as I am one close to you.* He thought of his star that was really a planet and wondered what it was like. Since it was his now, could he do whatever he wanted with it?

Again he spoke to the One. "When will I be able to do for my planet what you have done for this one?"

The One stopped and looked at the Dawn Star. His smile faded as He stared at him for a long while. He said nothing but continued to walk back toward the host.

He declared, "The evening has gone, and the morning is here."

The fourth day of creation was completed while the Dawn Star stood alone on the plain, away from the others.

19

THAT WHICH SWIMS, FLIES, AND RUNS

When the entire host of heaven returned to the holy temple after the fourth day of creation, the activities in the city of God continued as before. Michael and his ranks resumed their choreographed maneuvers, whose purpose could not yet be discerned. The reason for these drills were a mystery to the other hosts but accepted as a normal activity in the city of God.

The Dawn Star and his host could be found either with the tree of songs or in the tabernacle of praise. There seemed to be an unspoken sense of intentionality to their singing, as if they were all preparing for something.

The Spirit was often present wherever the Dawn Star and his host happened to be, whether in the tree or the tabernacle. She would silently observe and listen to the angelic voices and harmonies frequently with eyes closed. The Spirit would smile and nod in approval at the end of each piece.

In the tabernacle, the Dawn Star glided over to the where the Spirit leaned against a portion of the curved glass wall and stood beside her.

The Spirit spoke. "They are amazing," she said quietly as the host rehearsed a particularly intricate piece.

The Dawn Star smiled and said, "They are, aren't they?"

He looked upon them with great affection. His love for the host that had been given to him grew more and more in almost equal proportion to his love for his brother archangels. His love for the One still exceeded the boundaries of his affection for all other things.

As he stood listening to his host with the Spirit, the Dawn Star's thoughts went back to that early morning before dawn when the One had shown him his star and he had asked a question to which an answer had yet to be provided.

"When will I do for my planet as you have done for this one?" he asked again of the Spirit. "I want to know."

The Spirit looked at the Dawn Star and smiled. "Imagine a conversation between the land and the sea and the sky. The sea spends her days splashing against the rocks of the earth and cradling them in her embrace. She becomes weary of the earth's resistance to her. One day, she asks the sky, who watches over them both, 'When will I be the earth? I grow weary of splashing against the rock to no avail.' The sky looks down upon the sea and says, 'You are the sea and not the earth. You cannot become the earth because you were made to be the sea, nothing else. I am the sky, the land is the land, and you are the sea. That will never be changed.'"

The Dawn Star was confused by the Spirit's story. He could appreciate that the sky was the sky, the sea was the sea, and the land was the land, but it did little to answer the question on his mind.

The Spirit, seeing the Dawn Star's confusion, continued, "You are not the One. I am the uncreated. I am the One who has created all things from nothing. It is who I am, the Creator of the heavens and the Earth. To do what I do is to be me. There is no one like me and never shall there be. I am God, and you are the Dawn Star, an archangel of the host of heaven. That is what I created you to be. It is what I have ordained."

The Dawn Star took in the Spirit's words and made to respond, but the Spirit said gently, but with no less authority, "There will be no more talk of this."

The Dawn Star nodded and said, "Yes, my Lord."

With that, the Spirit gently touched the Dawn Star's face and left the tabernacle of praise.

At the dawn of the fifth day, upon the One's command, the host of heaven gathered all around the surface of the Earth to bear witness to the next step of creation. The One appeared before them carrying an enormous bound book tucked under His left arm. In His right hand was a scroll rolled up in two equal portions. Gabriel followed behind Him.

They came to the edge of one of the great seas of the Earth. The One turned and handed the scroll to Gabriel, who took it in both his arms and cradled it close to his chest. With the great bound book now in both hands, He opened it. Immediately a light shone from its pages, and the One turned and made a declaration to the host of heaven.

"Let all the waters on the Earth be filled with life. May they swarm with life, great and small. The fishes and the giant leviathans shall live and rule in all the seas!"

With that, the One turned and set the great book—the title of which, Gabriel had noticed, was *All That Live in the Water*—upon the surface of the sea and shoved it gently away from the shore. As it floated across the surface, it began to slowly sink and eventually disappeared beneath the surface of the sea. It continued to travel even while submerged, evidenced by a wake of light traveling behind it, stretching toward the horizon.

At one point, the wake of light that followed the book began to break off into smaller streams of light and branch off to take a different direction. When it reached the horizon, the surface of the sea was filled with swirling streams of light that eventually solidified and took the shape of the creatures they would become. Great schools of a vast variety of fish swam and swirled past the host on the shore. They reminded the Dawn Star of the lights in the night sky. It was as if they were the stars of the sea.

The host watched the movement of the fish and marveled at the variety of colors, shapes, and sizes. From time to time, they exclaimed to one another in sounds and words of wonder.

"Oh … Look at that one! … I saw that one in a book! … Did you see the one with the big fin? … Look how they all seem to move as one!"

Their observations were interrupted by a commotion halfway between the shore and the horizon, when creatures of enormous size began to propel themselves out of the water and then come crashing back down, creating white spikes of foam against the deep blue-green of the sea. This dance continued, and the entire ocean was transformed into a sea of waves and foam. The Dawn Star knew what joy felt like, but now as he stood on the shore with the One, his brothers, and the rest of the host, he knew what it looked like.

The One turned to Gabriel behind Him, stretched out His hand, and gestured to the scroll which he was clutching to his chest. Gabriel gave it to the Lord and stepped back.

The One took the scroll and declared, "It is time for the birds to take to the sky! This will be fun."

With that, He broke the seal, allowing the two even sides to unroll without restriction. Before it fell completely open, the One tossed it straight up into the air with both hands. There it unfurled to its full length and flapped and undulated as the wind took it farther up into the sky.

When the unfurled scroll reached a certain height, the One looked up and began to laugh with His head tilted back. At first it began with a giggle and then low chuckles. It continued on until it turned into a loud, joyful guffaw. Just as God's laughter in the beginning had broken the light apart and scattered it to the far reaches of the universe, it shattered against the scroll floating in the sky, tearing it and scattering it into a myriad of pieces. But they were no longer pieces of parchment; they had now taken the form of winged creatures in scores of colors and sizes.

As had the fish in the sea, the birds swirled, soared, and darted through the sky, changing direction in the blink of an eye. To the delight of the host, the air was filled with the sound of their chirps, squawks, whistles, and songs.

"Sing with them!" came the voice of the One over the commotion of the birds.

At once, the Dawn Star and his host began to sing the songs about the birds they each had been assigned. When the voices of the host were added to the songs of the birds, which had previously been not much more than cacophonous noise, the immediate effect brought a kind of order to the winged creatures' whistles, chirps, squawks, songs. It was like instruments in an orchestra coming into tune with one another.

The Dawn Star closed his eyes and smiled as he listened carefully to the joyful noise that his host and the creatures in the air made together. He thought to himself that once the sky had been silent and the sea had been still, but now they were both bursting with life. With that thought, another song from the tree burst upon his memory, and he opened his mouth and added it to the others already filling the air. It was the anthem celebrating new life coming into the world in the form of the birds of the air and the fish of the sea. It was a perfect counterpoint to that which was already being sung.

Amid the music, the One stepped out onto the sea and started to walk away from the shore and rise into the air at the same time. As he rose, the birds began to gather around and above Him, and the creatures of the sea gathered beneath Him. At the close of the songs, some of the birds were perched on and around Him; others could be seen hovering in the glory that emanated from the Lord. A great leviathan breached the surface, providing with his broad snout a place for the One to stand upon.

From the shore, the Dawn Star and the rest of the host watched as Creator and creation began to converse with one another. Though He was not speaking directly to them, they could hear what God was saying. He was speaking plainly as if He were talking to friends, to the Dawn Star, or to one of the other members of the heavenly host.

"Now all of you are just the first of many … Go and fill the sea, the earth, and the sky with your children. You are all so good. You are all beautiful. Let your beauty be seen everywhere, from the depths of the oceans and every corner of the world. Now go!" With that, the newly formed creation exploded away from the One who created them to do what He had commanded.

When the Lord had returned to the shore where host waited for Him, the sun was dipping below the western horizon.

"This is good," declared the One.

The fifth day of creation was complete.

The Dawn Star, Michael, and Gabriel stood in the open cathedral windows of the temple, looking down upon the Earth. To the three it felt very close to them. It seemed as if the land, sea, and sky were a part of the city of God itself. It was like the two, though very different from one another, were always meant to be with one another. As the three archangels watched, some birds flew so high that it looked like they would perch on the holy temple itself. But, not made for the rarified atmosphere of heaven, they banked and drifted away.

While watching the birds descend toward the Earth, the Dawn Star had a thought to join them in flight. As he shuffled his feet toward the edge of the temple, he hesitated, thinking for a moment that it would be an intrusion.

But as he stepped away from the edge, the voice of the One behind him said, "What are you waiting for? Go. Enjoy yourself … the three of you … have fun."

The three archangels looked at one another and in unison jumped, leaped, and dove down toward the great flock of birds. When they reached them, the birds scattered, not out of fright but more out of a sense of curiosity for the creatures that had joined them in their flight.

Michael turned on his back in the air and had the joy of several birds landing on his broad chest and outstretched arms and legs as he carried them through the sky. Gabriel looked as if he were standing in the middle of the air as flocks of birds swirled around him. He seemed to be in conversation with them, for his gentle voice could be heard intermittently through the songs, squawks, and trills of the birds around him.

The Dawn Star began singing the moment he took to the air. Sometimes he flew alone, only to be joined by different kinds of birds from time to time. He sang the song of each kind of bird he happened to be flying with at the moment.

Again, as in many times before, overwhelming joy washed over him in waves as he marveled at the wonder and beauty of the One's creation, not just the birds but all of it—the land, the sea, the sky, the fishes, and the endless shades of green that framed the Earth. His appreciation included the sun and the moon and the millions of stars and planets in the sky. To think that all of this was created from the nothingness of the waters and the imagination and heart of God, the Lord, the One. The Dawn Star realized he was really rejoicing over the fact that he was part of it all, and according to the One, he was an important, integral part. With that knowledge, he sang even louder every song that he had learned from the tree, all of which spoke of the glories of God's creation.

When the Dawn Star came to the end of one of the pieces, he looked down from the sky to see the One standing in a meadow, surrounded by grass and flowers. He was looking up with His arms outstretched, beckoning them to join Him. The three archangels alighted in the meadow surrounding the One. The rest of the host of heaven gathered in and around the holy temple to observe what would come next.

Where the One stood was a bare patch of brown earth. Looking around at the three archangels and up to the host in the holy temple, He said, "A new day is upon us! Let's finish this. Let all the rest of creation come forth!"

When these words from the One were spoken, they traveled all the way from the Earth, through the temple, and into the palace of all things, specifically into the room of God's word. At the sound of His voice, all the images and illustrations from the books and the constant motion around the room began to spill out almost at once into the great hall, out the jade doors, and up the golden staircase that led to the holy temple. They traveled through the temple, around the host crowding the cathedral windows, and out and down to the One waiting for them on Earth.

The One, surrounded by His glory, saw the images of His creation descend upon Him, and He welcomed them with outstretched arms. The images were soon absorbed into the glory of God, making it shine even brighter. The Dawn Star and his brothers observed the One smile in deep satisfaction as He paused to take in all that just happened.

He stood quiet and still on the patch of bare earth in the meadow filled with flowers. Then He knelt on one knee, stretched His hand flat to the ground, bent His head, and spoke softly to the earth itself: "Now it is your turn!"

At these words, the earth beneath His hand began to glow with a light similar to the lights and colors of the swirling images from the room of God's word. For quite some time, the One remained kneeling, His hand held flat against the earth. When the light faded from the ground, the Dawn Star observed Him speaking words he could not hear. This was a moment, he thought, that belonged only to the One and all that would come next.

After this moment, the One stood up straight and waited. A smile crossed His glory-filled face when a low rumbling vibration was felt beneath the Dawn Star's feet. Michael and Gabriel felt it as well. The rumble grew in strength and volume until the ground itself was shaking. Instinctively, the three took to the air while the One stayed where He stood on the ground.

"What is happening?" the Dawn Star asked.

"Something wonderful," He said. "Just wait. You'll see."

With that, as if on cue, the entire meadow erupted with swarms of color as winged insects of all kinds filled the air around them … like living jewels. The light of the sun and the glory of God reflected off their wings and small, shiny bodies. They reminded the Dawn Star of some of the colors he had seen inside the holy temple.

All eyes were fixed on the ballet being performed before them. Even the One, with a broad smile on His face, watched them, transfixed by their dance as if it were a pleasant surprise. The Dawn Star was well aware that this was no surprise because he knew that every flit and flutter, every rise and fall the insect's movement, was meticulously choreographed by the Lord Himself long before any living thing came into being.

The swarms took on a character of their own as each sought out their own kind. As these various groups of insects assembled together, some of them rose farther into the air and departed the boundaries of the meadow. Many of those that remained in the meadow fluttered up to the hovering archangels.

When one of them happened to land on top of Gabriel's hand, he smiled and said, "Butterflies. These are butterflies."

"So this is what a butterfly looks like," the Dawn Star said, smiling. Looking up in the direction of the temple, where he knew his host would be watching, he said, "Sing it Allegro!"

With that, Allegro's clear tenor voice rang down from heaven as he sang the lyrical tune of the butterfly, the first song given to him by the Dawn Star from the tree of songs. The flight pattern of all the butterflies seemed to match the light bouncy rhythm of Allegro's voice and song.

The One looked at the Dawn Star, smiled, and said, "Very good."

When the song ended, the edges of the meadow at the tree line came alive with movement as a variety of animals began to make their way from the shadows of the forest into the light of the meadow. Some ran together in herds. Some walked in stately fashion, slowly taking in their surroundings. The tall trees on the perimeter shook as some of the newly formed creatures strode into the meadow with large, slow, heavy steps.

As the day continued, the Dawn Star and the rest of the host observed a continuous variety of creatures make their way onto the meadow to where the One stood. Some ran, most walked, others crawled, and some meandered slowly toward the One, nibbling on the grasses of the meadow as they went. All the animals that made themselves known eventually made it to where the Lord stood, and He greeted each with an outstretched hand or a nuzzle to their heads. Each gesture was gentle and loving.

The Dawn Star recognized many of them from the images that swirled around the room of God's word. From his place hovering above the field of grass and flowers, he observed that nothing compared to the beauty and majesty of those images now given breath, life, and movement in the flesh. The sheer variety left him breathless and filled with wonder … It seemed to have affected the One in the same way as He looked slowly around and took in all that He had created this day. The joy for what He made radiated from Him like ripples in still water, which was felt all the way to the temple of heaven itself.

The Lord opened His mouth and spoke. "You are all so good! Now go live your lives, all of you. Fill the Earth, every part of it."

Upon that command, all the creatures lifted their voices in roars, trumpeting, joyful howling, bleats, mews, barks, buzzes, and so many other sounds.

"Sing with them, Dawn Star! Sing their song!" said the One.

Without a moment's hesitation, a song from the tree came to his memory, the song of the living creatures, and he sang, "All creatures of the One, our Lord and King. Lift all your voices and sing … sing … sing. Alleluia! Alleluia! Alleluia!"

At this point in the song, the entire host of heaven was singing the anthem, with the host of the Dawn Star providing the harmonies. The whole Earth seemed to be filled with all the voices of heaven and Earth. Their alleluias echoed through the forests, mountains, plains, and sea even after the anthem was complete: "Alleluia, alleluia, alleluia …"

OUT OF THE DUST

As the hymn came to a close, the variety of creatures began to scatter and leave the field, some with great leaps, others at a dead run, and still others lumbering back to from where they had come without a care in the world. Soon the meadow was empty except for the One and the three archangels hovering above it.

The sun cast the long shadows of a late afternoon when the three brothers joined the One on the ground. He turned to them and said, "It is time for the beloved."

At the sound of those words, the Dawn Star felt a surge of emotion come over him. Ever since he had come into being, the beloved had been the central focus of almost everything that was a part of the kingdom of heaven and, for that matter, the whole of creation. He recalled the One declaring to him that the Earth would be the home of the beloved. He smiled when he remembered the voices and laughter in the purple firmament at the top of the great hall, and he relived the deep emotion of the eternal song of the beloved. Now the moment of the beloved was upon them, and they would be witnesses to their creation.

God knelt down to the ground and touched it tenderly as if something that was not yet there had already come into existence. They watched as tears from the One, overwhelmed with emotion, fell to the ground and sank into the earth. All was quiet and still, until the Lord spoke.

"Leave Me," he said calmly.

Before the three brothers could fully comprehend the command, they found themselves back up in the temple with the rest of the host of heaven. The Dawn Star made his way through the crowd of host toward the opening of the cathedral window. The sight that lay before them at the edge of temple was the meadow with the One kneeling in the dust, just as when He had dismissed them. But the view was at a distance far greater than they had watched from on previous days of creation. They were able to see the One's general movements, but the details were kept from them.

The Dawn Star made to go down for a closer look, but he got no farther than a few feet from the temple's edge. This was as close as he could get to witness this aspect of creation.

An odd feeling came over the Dawn Star as he was made to keep his distance. He had been allowed to personally witness every detail of the formation and birth of Michael and Gabriel. He had been present at the formation of the heavenly host and the setting of the foundations of the world and the entire universe. But at the formation of the crown of creation, the beloved, he was kept at a distance. He had never yet experienced the One's desire for privacy. This clearly was one of those moments, and the Lord would be sharing it with only Himself.

Even from the vantage point he was given in heaven, the Dawn Star observed the Three that made up the One converse with each other, just as before his brother archangels had come into being. Then the One spoke in the plural voice of the Three, loud enough to be heard from heaven.

"It is time for the beloved! They will be made in Our image, a reflection of Our nature, a reflection of Our heart. They will be made to be as one, male and female. A man and a woman. All that has been created will be theirs. They will care for it as I care for them. They will be the shepherds of all living things!"

The excitement and anticipation of what would come next was felt throughout all the host gathered at the temple in heaven. No feelings, however, were stronger than those felt by the Dawn Star himself. He had seen the idea of them, sung the song dedicated to them, previewed the world that would be their home. Almost from the time of his own creation, he had been anticipating the coming of the beloved … and now it was here. He watched almost breathlessly as the One once again turned His attention to the bare patch of ground now made wet by His tears of deep emotion.

The Dawn Star was surprised to see the glory of God, which was always about Him, seem to fade in its vibrancy, as if He were trying not to stand out so much in contrast to His creation. Instead of a contrast, there was now a gentle blending with it, creating a picture of close harmony between Himself and the work of His hands.

The One dug His hands into the clay made from the dust and His tears of joy, and lifted great chunks of it to His breast, which he began to shape and form into the desired image He had in His heart for the beloved. From the clay, details of a head, torso, and limbs began to appear. The figure was smaller than the Dawn Star and the rest of the host. Its color was that of the earth from which it was formed, brown and ruddy in hue. The hair on its head was dark brown to black, framing a young face. Its eyes were closed as if it were sleeping.

The Dawn Star watched the One cradle the completed figure lovingly in His arms for some time and was aware that everything in heaven and on Earth had become completely silent. It reminded him of the time just before the host was created in the holy temple, when a deep, breathless quiet preceded what would come next. Like that time before, nothing stirred or interrupted this holy moment. No one felt the need or compulsion to sing or speak or even move.

It was a moment of complete stillness … until the Lord bent His head toward the face of the figure and kissed it. The only sound heard at that point was the breath of God going into that which was once just a figure made of clay … followed by a soft sound of "yaaaah" as the figure took its first breath.

The Dawn Star heard Gabriel declare in almost a whispered sense of awe, "The first human being, a man."

The only indication that the figure, this "human being" lying in the arms of the One, was a living soul was the rise and fall of its chest as it breathed in and out. Occasionally an arm or a leg would move, giving more proof of life within it. Beyond that, there was not much else, which puzzled the Dawn Star.

When the other creatures were created, the birds, the fish, the animals of the land, and even the insects had seemed to burst forth with a joyful energy of praise and gratitude for the gift of being alive from the moment they were alive. The Dawn Star thought back to the moment of his own creation when he had heard the One say, "Open your eyes." The joy of that moment had overwhelmed him so much that he had barely been able to contain his emotions. If this was indeed the beginning of the beloved, the Dawn Star found it initially to be a disappointment.

As the shadows of the afternoon grew longer, the One gently laid the figure on the ground, where it remained still except for the steady movement of its chest as it continued to breath easily. Its eyes remained closed. The Dawn Star had no understanding of sleep or the need for it, but it was something all living creatures would participate in on a regular basis.

While the figure slept, the One touched its side. The details of what He was doing could not easily be determined, but it was clear that something was taken from the figure, which now lay in the palm of His hand.

The Dawn Star, along with rest of the host, observed the Lord speaking gently to the whitish object in His hand, though details of what was being said could not be discerned. As He spoke, the simple object began to grow in size until a torso with limbs and a head were clearly visible. Eventually another human figure lay in the arms of the One, slightly smaller and with the same coloring. But where the first figure was more angular in shape, the new one was softer in body, with subtle curves.

The Dawn Star glanced at Gabriel as he said, "A woman." As if responding to Gabriel's declaration, they all heard the One say, "The beloved are complete."

As with the first figure, the Lord leaned down to kiss the one lying in his arms. Its longer hair framed a delicate face. Once again, the breath of God was heard from heaven, followed by another "yaaaah" as the new creation took its first breath and continued to breath easily. Everything remained still and silent. Nothing stirred except the One when he bent down and picked up the sleeping man while still holding the woman.

While both were still, the One cradled them in His arms. He then stood, turned, and began walking toward the eastern edge of the meadow, taking the man and woman with Him. As He walked, the place that was once a bare patch of ground in the middle of meadow was covered with grass and flowers as if they had always been there.

The host, along with the Dawn Star, Michael, and Gabriel, watched the One carry his beloved across the field and walk into the trees surrounding the meadow as the last shadows of day disappeared into evening. The only indication of light, besides the stars in the sky, was the glory of the One peeking through the limbs and branches of trees. The evening was quiet except for the sound of voices talking. No words could be heard, but the conversation sounded pleasant.

Again the Dawn Star was struck by how relatively unremarkable the creation of the beloved was. In his mind, they were far from the "crown of creation" they had been lauded to be. Perhaps the One was not finished with them yet and what was happening in the woods, away from the view of the host, was the completion of their creation process. But just as the Dawn Star came to that conclusion, the One appeared in the holy temple.

As the Dawn Star and the rest of the host looked at Him, He said, "They're sleeping … The whole world is sleeping. After all, it's been a long day. It's time to rest."

The One turned and looked down at His creation—the stars and planets of the universe, the green earth, the sea, the sky, all the creatures that ran and walked and swam and flew … and the beloved.

"It is finished," He said. "It is all done, and it is all good."

THE SEVENTH DAY

The Dawn Star and the rest of the host only knew it as Sabbath, the day of rest. It would come after the work of creation was complete. The Dawn Star had been preparing for this day almost from the beginning.

All the preparation by his host had been leading up to this day, for on this day, God would rest and enjoy what He had made. Everything designed by the One—which up until now had only been seen in the books, scrolls, and charts in the room of God's word—was now laid out before them … Everything was set and in its place, from the tiniest blade of grass to the tallest tree. From the smallest organism to the largest leviathan in the sea. From the atomic particles to galaxies so enormous it would take thousands of millennia to arrive at their center. Everything in creation, seen or unseen, was there, ready to live and exist in symphony together. This would be a day of celebration!

As all in the Earth and the heavens was in its place, so also was the host of heaven. The city of God was quiet and empty of all its citizens, for all were present somewhere in creation, ready to do what they had been preparing to do. There were no longer three different sets of hosts; they were all one on this day. They all mingled together, put completely under the charge of the Dawn Star.

The holy temple was the place where the fullness of creation could be observed in its entirety. Opposite the great doors of the temple, which opened out to the city of God and the endless golden vista, all the beauty, color, intricacies, and majesty of creation was framed by the three cathedral openings. The Lord in all His glory stood in the center window and gazed upon all He had made in silence. The One was alone. As He was before anything else had come into being. There were no sounds from the city, no sound of voices singing or in conversation, no sound of movement of any kind. It was that velvety silence that, as before, served as a prelude to what would come. It was the in-between moment of what was next. It was the space between breaths. It was holy.

And then God stepped out into creation to begin the day.

In the predawn darkness, the Dawn Star could be seen hovering above the eastern horizon with his morning star visible just above his shoulder. They were the vision of a celestial duet that was about to unfold. He was shining bright against the velvety background of the night sky. Those who observed that moment and were familiar with the Dawn Star's golden aura would say on this day it was different in brightness and splendor; only the glory of the One shone brighter. All the attention of heaven and Earth was turned onto the brilliant figure of the Dawn Star … and then he began to sing.

The hymn of the new day started out as a sustained singular note just as a ribbon of lavender and then pink appeared below the Dawn Star's feet. As the ribbon of color changed to orange and then yellow, the one note grew in intensity and volume. One note became a melody of several notes, and those notes were joined to words.

The Dawn Star's voice was all that was heard as the sun peaked above the horizon, as the Earth rotated to gradually give way to the fullness of the sun's glory. At one point, the sun was directly behind the Dawn Star, making them both appear as one bright object in the morning sky.

As the One looked upon the first of His creation, His heart filled with even more joy than was already there. This moment was unfolding just as He had foreseen, long before the plans and foundations of creation were put into place, He looked upon this moment as if He were seeing and experiencing it for the first time. Even though the Lord was responsible for every element captured in the moment. He never loved his Dawn Star more than He did at this very moment.

As the sun continued to climb into the sky and separate itself from the Dawn Star to become its own entity again, the hymn expanded and was joined by other voices of the heavenly host. That which had begun as a solo expanded into a duet, a trio, a quartet, until it was a full chorus of voices adding different parts and harmonies to the piece. Every member of the heavenly host stationed throughout creation was singing the anthem of the completion of creation. "It Is Finished" was the theme sung throughout the hymn:

> It is finished. God's work is done!
> Rejoice O earth and sky and sea.
> Let all creation now declare the glory of the One!

At a certain point, the Lord had made His way down to the large meadow from which the beloved were formed. He stood with his arms outstretched and head thrown back, taking in the concert of the angels. His glory grew to such a point that it stretched beyond the boundaries of the meadow and through the forest surrounding it.

The glory of God continued to spread throughout the day until there was not anything made by the hand of God that had not been touched personally by it.

In turn, as each aspect of creation was touched by the presence of the One, all creation began to make its own joyful noise. The winds blew through the trees, creating a harmonic humming sound. The breezes caused the various limbs and branches to crack together, providing percussion to the music surrounding creation.

Just as the music began, the two figures of the beloved emerged from the forest and made their way out to the center of the meadow where the One stood. The Lord looked down on them and smiled as they took their places on each side of Him to listen. As the hymn ended, a host of angelic beings circled the great meadow high above the forest's tree line and added their voices to the climax of the song.

At the end of the first song, with barely a breath between them, another song began with the lower voices of the heavenly host chanting and humming a deep, rhythmic, harmonic "*thrum, thrum, thrum, thrum*." Other voices from the host added melodic staccato harmonies that blended into an additional melody that felt as if it were an introduction to a greater melodic theme that was waiting to make its appearance. At a certain point, the voices ceased as if responding to an unseen cue. There was a moment of complete stillness until a new movement of music took its place.

As it began, with the Dawn Star's voice leading the soft sweeping chorus of treble voices, the animals that had been formed on the last day of creation began to enter the great meadow from all sides. They all seemed to move toward the center where the One stood with the beloved. They came slowly and deliberately, without hesitation.

In turn, the birds of the air appeared in the sky and approached them in whirling, sweeping clouds of color. As the animals drew nearer to where the Lord stood, birds began to land on the head, shoulders, and outstretched hands of the One as well as the beloved. As they landed and took off again, others quickly replaced them. At one point, the figures disappeared from view because of the great flock, except for the glory of God, which surrounded them all. As the other animals approached, the birds dispersed as if to say, "We've had ours. Now it's your turn."

The great cats arrived at the center first and began to rub their bodies affectionately against the One as He reached down and scratched them behind the ears. The subsequent low purrs of pleasure from the cats joined with the songs of the heavenly chorus already in progress. At one point, a large striped cat stood on its hind legs, knocked the man to the ground, and then lay on top of him and began to lick his face. The man laughed so continually at this that he was barely able to breath as he moved his head in a vain attempt to avoid the cat's tongue. Clearly it was a great game between man and beast, with no clear winner.

The woman, not be left out, threw herself with glee on top of the cat, producing a sudden "oof!" from the man at the bottom of the pile. The One, amid His own crowd of felines, began to laugh at the joyful, roiling scene taking place at His feet.

The song of the heavenly host continued through the morning as other varieties of animals came to the center to greet the One who made them and the beloved. The man and the woman began to mingle with the other creatures as the One looked on.

As he led the chorus from his position above the meadow, the Dawn Star observed the scene below him. The beloved were running with the creatures, climbing on them, and wrestling with them, which none of the animals seemed to mind. They were all playing together as their way of celebrating the completion of creation. The song for each creature was sung by the member of his host to whom it was given. Even as the other animals made their way into the meadow, their particular melodies could be heard until eventually hundreds of songs were being sung at once, and the Dawn Star was the conductor.

There was not a hint of disharmony in the music being expressed at the same time. There was no discord, no confusion of sound. Even when each animal added its own particular roar, howl, trumpet, screech, song, or bark, it all fit into a perfect symphony of music … and the One enjoyed it all as He moved and danced among them.

The Dawn Star came to the realization that it was for this moment that he was created … It was for this moment that he was entrusted with all the music that grew from the tree of songs. He was not their composer, but he had been given the gift, the ability, to see how they all fit together as one beautiful song of creation.

As these thoughts washed over him, he rose farther into the air and began to spin just as he had the first time he opened his eyes on the One. Like that first time, his arms were thrown out to his sides, and ribbons of light came streaming out and spiraling around him. It was pure joy that he was experiencing, just it had been the first time in the temple with the One. He was lost in the euphoria of it.

There was a moment that the music faded to a stop. All the participants in the symphony turned their gazes, including the One, toward the dance of the Dawn Star. As they watched, they heard the unmistakable beauty of the Dawn Star's voice singing a doxology.

"Praise God from whom all blessings flow. Praise Him all creatures here below. Praise Him above ye heavenly host …"

After the chorus had ended, the Dawn Star looked in the Lord's direction and mouthed a silent "thank you." The One smiled and nodded in reply.

At that, with a wave of his arms the Dawn Star indicated that the symphony should continue, which it did, as if there had been no interruption whatsoever.

As if on cue, the glory of the One began to expand as He rose into the air. The birds seemed to gather at once around the Lord until they were completely engulfed by the glory of God. The songs of each individual species of bird added their unique sounds to the symphonic mix already in progress.

When the sun had reached its zenith in its course of the day, the One in His glory high above the meadow began to move away from land toward the nearest coast and eventually out to sea. As the glory of God moved across the border of land and sea, the ocean began to rise up in enormous waves to greet the One as He came. They seemed to connect and gather as white foamy hands in applause. They added a crashing jubilant percussion to the music of the day. Just as the land had its say in the celebration of creation, it was now the sea's turn.

It was as if the seas had been waiting anxiously for the One to make Himself known. At the Lord's appearance, along with the waves, the oceans began to boil with life. Silver shoals of fish reflected sparkling light like jewels just beneath the surface. A great number of larger fish breeched the surface and propelled themselves into the air, wiggling their tails and bodies in a kinetic dance of joy.

Shortly after the Lord's appearance, the Dawn Star moved his company to the seas and began a second movement of the symphony already in progress. His host sang the songs of every creature in the sea. The creatures of the sea added their own unique songs, sounds, or clicks to the proceedings.

Then with a great laugh, the One began to race across the surface of the ocean. As the Lord passed, great leviathans breached the surface and splashed back down, producing great lacy curtains of foam. The One was joined in His race across the sea by pods of sea mammals moving in and out of the water like a thousand hills in constant motion. From time to time, the One dove beneath the surface, followed by His glory, only to emerge with more animals caught up in His wake.

The Dawn Star and his company followed the path of the One across the seas. He was the only archangel to do so. It was apparent that Gabriel, Michael, and their perspective hosts held station elsewhere in creation. The privilege of accompanying the One on this journey was his alone, along with his host. They got to witness the sheer joy of the One. He was lost in it.

As he observed the actions of the One, he came to understand that perhaps this was what the Lord had been waiting for. This was the reason for creation. This was the reason for the beloved … for all of it. The Dawn Star was witnessing firsthand God enjoying what He had made.

The sun was making its descent to the western horizon when the One returned to the meadow and the beloved, who were waiting for Him. The current movement of the creation symphony began to fade as the sun disappeared from the horizon. When a dark ribbon of pink was the only visible sign of the sun's presence, the One lay down in the meadow with the man and the woman on either side of Him, looking into the night sky as more and more stars came into view. They watched the Dawn Star and his host ascend into the heavens like shooting stars in reverse, until their bright figures were lost among the brightness of the other stars. The evening had completely engulfed them when they heard a distant sound from above. The voice of the Dawn Star.

"Here it comes," the One said, not hiding the delight in His voice.

With that, it was as if everything in the cosmos moved closer into view so that each planet, nebula, star cluster, and galaxy could be seen almost at once. The beloved inhaled sharply at the phenomenon. They both instinctively reached out a hand in a vain attempt to touch them. The Lord chuckled beside them.

The Earth was a small blue marble from the Dawn Star's position in space when he began the last movement of the symphony. Even at this distance, he knew his song would be heard by those observing from the Earth.

When the Dawn Star had finished the introduction, his host began to sing together all the songs of the stars and planets at once. Just as with the others of creation, there was no dissonance. Nothing was out of tune or disharmonious. The sound reflected the unity in which the universe operated almost from the moment it had come into existence.

The planets and the stars seemed to shine a bit brighter when their individual songs were sung. It went like that for a while, to the delight of those observing from below. At some point the three in meadow—the man, the woman, and the One—rose and began to dance together beneath the stars, twirling and leaping in a celebration of creation.

The music came to a pause, directed by the Dawn Star. With a nod of his head, a high, clear, singular voice could be heard coming from deep inside a nebula. It was the unmistakable voice of Gloria, the smallest of the Dawn Star's host. Only two voices among God's heavenly citizens were able to catch the attention of almost everyone who heard them: the Dawn Star's and Gloria's. The song of the nebula was a fitting climax to the songs of the stars. It contained within its melody notes of mystery and majesty. It was an invitation to discover more, to discover, if at all possible, the secrets of all the universe.

As the rest of the host took up the melody of the nebula, Gloria found herself beside the Dawn Star. The rest of the host clustered around him as if they were their own constellation with the brightness of the Dawn Star at its very center. Together they began to finish the last movement of creation's symphony.

The attention of every living thing on Earth was turned to that shining spot in the heavens—every creature on land and sea, every angelic being left on Earth, the beloved, and even the One, who was filled with as much love in this moment as anyone could imagine. His day of rest was coming to an end as the last notes of music faded and the pale light of the moon began to peak over the eastern horizon.

The One gathered the beloved into His arms as they faded off to sleep, walked them to the garden just outside the meadow, and gently laid them down. When He returned, the night sky had reverted back to its original formation, with nebulas and galaxies hidden by the vastness of space. The Earth was left quiet and still as the moon shone softly upon it.

Creation was finished and celebrated. Now it was time for all of it to live and become what the Lord had intended it be.

From His holy temple, the One looked down upon all that He had made and declared, "It is good."

PART 2

IN THE GARDEN

After the completion of creation, the One settled the beloved into the garden He had provided for them. Though the Earth was filled with all manner of vegetation spread across the various regions, it seemed as if every species of plant, especially that of the fruit-bearing kind, were represented in the garden. This was to be the home of the man and the woman. The One called it Eden, "a place of pleasure," for everything within the boundaries of the garden was intended to be a delight to the beloved. Which it was.

Every day the beloved explored their home with joy and abandon, running through the woods, playing hiding games, swimming in crystal clear pools throughout the garden, climbing high into trees and peeking through the uppermost bower to survey from above the paradise that was their home. Every new experience the man and the woman shared together was always under the watchful presence of the One, who often joined in their games. Every day was spent at what could only be described as playing. Their laughter, along with that of the Lord, became the constant song of the garden.

The Dawn Star and the rest of God's heavenly host were free to venture between heaven and creation as they pleased. From heaven's point of view, angels seemed to fill the Earth as much as the creatures did. Each seemed to have a particular fondness for the different aspects of creation.

Gabriel had an interest for the sea and all that lived there. Often he could be found on a promontory by the ocean, leaning against a tree while studying the volumes of books from the room of God's word that seemed to pertain to his specific interest.

On the northern edge of the garden was a stand of large rocks that towered above it. This was Michael's preferred position. From there he could observe much of what went on in the garden. He had instructed his host to take up positions around its boundaries. They and Michael stood a vigilant watch around Eden.

From the Dawn Star's own host, Gloria favored the cosmos and being among the stars. Allegro was fascinated with the small and tiny representations of creation. He could often be found surrounded by jewel-winged insects, especially butterflies.

For the Dawn Star, it was the beloved themselves who held his interest, more out of curiosity than anything else. After he sang in the song of the day's dawning, which he had every morning since the completion of creation, he would follow the One into the garden and observe His interactions with the man and the woman from a short distance.

It became clear that the presence of the Dawn Star, and the rest of the host, were unnoticed by the humans. All the other creatures seemed to be fully aware of the angelic presence, but the man and the woman were indifferent to them. They were, however, fully aware of the Lord whenever He was in their midst. They greeted Him each day with joy and delight as they all found a new game to play or activity to discover. The Dawn Star observed that the man and the woman operated within the garden in unabashed freedom, doing whatever seemed to please them and going wherever they wished to go without restrictions. The one exception was the tree that grew in the middle of the garden.

When the One first brought the beloved to Eden, He walked around with them, showing them all the wonders contained within it, especially two trees in particular. The Dawn Star observed intently the Lord's interactions with the man and the woman regarding their responsibilities to the garden, especially to the two trees.

As usual, the man and the woman, who the One called Adam and Eve, looked upon Him and listened with awe and wonder. At one point He indicated for them to sit with Him on the ground at equal distance between the two trees. This reminded the Dawn Star of when he had sat with the One on the floor of the great hall, just before He showed him the tree of songs, in the time before his brothers and before the host. The memory warmed his heart. Now God was sitting again with those He loved and was speaking of a tree.

The One looked intently at them both and spoke gently. "This garden is yours. I created it for you."

Adam and Eve broke eye contact with the One and looked around over the Lord's shoulder and behind them. They looked up and to the side, trying to take in every wonder of the garden at once.

"All this is ours?" Adam asked.

The One nodded His affirmation.

"We thought it belonged to you?" questioned Eve.

"My dear beloved, everything I have is yours."

"Everything?"

"All that is in this garden belongs to you to do with as you please."

The man and the woman did not fully comprehend what the One was telling them.

"I gave you this place as your home. Tend to it, care for it … make it beautiful," said the One, smiling.

Eve said, "It is already beautiful!"

The Lord smiled at her. "Let's see what you can do with the place."

The Dawn Star took in every word of the conversation and found himself perplexed by the One's words to the man and the woman. The garden belonged to them? They could do anything they wanted with it? Make it beautiful? What could they do that God had not already done? He hoped to speak to the One about these questions and more regarding the beloved.

The One continued, "And I want you to take care of all the animals in the garden."

At that news, the Dawn Star saw them smile broadly and clap with delight. He remembered how actively they had played with all the creatures on that seventh day, the day of celebration.

"And I want you to name them."

They looked at the One in slight confusion.

The One said, "You are a man and a woman. You are Adam," He said, pointing at the man. Then to the woman, He said, "You are Eve. That's who you are. I have a name, and all the host in heaven have names. The animals need names."

"What should we name them?" they asked.

The Lord said, "Anything you want."

They both looked at one another and tried sounding out words and syllables that came to them without any particular animal in mind.

"*All-lee-font*," Eve sounded out slowly and then laughed at the name she had come up with.

Adam responded with a name of his own: "*Bo-no-bo*." He

over-exaggerated the shape of his mouth, forming his lips into perfect *o*'s on each syllable, which caused Eve to erupt into a torrent of giggles and then quickly imitate the comical face he made.

She sat upright and said, "*Bo-no-bo!*"

Adam laughed in turn and said, "*All-lee-font!*"

They fell on their backs, letting the rolls of laughter take over the moment, and the One laughed with them.

The Dawn Star looked on, perplexed. He had already sung the song for each of the animals whose names they supposedly just made up. Didn't the One already know what they were to be and what they would be named? Yet He acted as if it were their idea. Why didn't the Lord just tell them what the names were?

Then, as if the Lord had heard the questions forming in the Dawn Star's mind, he heard the voice of the One in his head say, "What kind of fun would that be?" The Dawn Star looked up to see the One looking back at him over His shoulder and then indicate the beloved laughing on the ground. "This is better," he heard Him say.

When the laughter was over, the One continued. "I want you to know that all the fruit that grow on the plants and trees you are free to eat and enjoy."

Their eyes grew wide with delight and excitement.

Adam pointed to the large, bright, flowering tree to his right. "Even that one?"

The One said, "Yes. Even the Tree of Life when it starts bearing fruit. You may enjoy the fruit of that tree as well."

Eve looked to her left and asked, "What about that one?" She indicated a tree that grew in a deep, shady part of the garden.

The One became still. His tone was firm and quiet when He spoke. "That is the tree of the knowledge of good and evil. I ask that you not eat the fruit from that tree or even go near it."

They both looked at the tree.

The One continued "… for if you were to eat from that tree …" He paused. "You would die."

They both looked at him, not comprehending fully the meaning of His words.

Adam spoke up. "Father, what does it mean … would die?"

"To die means you would stop living. It means that you would not be with me anymore forever …" The One paused and looked at them. The joy that was ever so present in the One barely registered on His face when He said, "… and I would not be with you."

They sat silently taking in the full meaning of the Lord's words. Suddenly, Eve stood and flung herself into the One and held on to Him tightly.

"We don't want to be without You," she said as she clung to Him.

Adam joined her and said, "We always want to be with You."

The One embraced them both, chuckled, and said, "I know, and I always want you to be with Me." He held them away from Him and looked at them gravely. "But you must listen to Me about this and obey Me … Do not touch that tree ever, or you will lose everything. You will never be the same again. Nothing will be the same again. It will be gone forever."

The One stood, offered His hand to them, and led them away from the two trees as He continued to speak to them. "Come. Let me show you some more," he said, His warmth and joy returning to Him in full measure.

Even from the distance at which he observed the One's interaction with the man and the woman, the Dawn Star sensed a change in the Lord's demeanor. He spoke with authority, yet it was coupled with a sense of pleading that seemed to underline His words as He commanded them regarding the tree of knowledge of good and evil.

It was as if He were commanding all of creation as well, if it was listening. Even the Dawn Star felt the power and authority of the One's words.

As the Lord walked away with the beloved, the Dawn Star moved closer to the tree, intending to keep a safe distance from it. It looked to be a smaller, duller version of his tree of songs, complete with golden fruit of its own but without the innate brightness that distinguished the light fruit of the tree. To him the tree held no appeal. In contrast to the other splendors in the garden, it seemed quite unremarkable. Nothing about it seemed dangerous or ominous to him.

But a question lingered in his mind. Why did the One plant such a tree in the first place?

It was then that the Dawn Star became aware of the Spirit's voice inside his mind, in answer to his unspoken question.

"It is here to give them a choice. It is their greatest gift, or it can be their greatest curse. The beloved are free to obey me if they so choose. I will not take that away from them."

The Dawn Star acknowledged the answer given but found himself still feeling uneasy, unsatisfied. With so much at stake, with the implication that all of creation would hang in the balance, why would the Lord take that risk with them? It was not often that the Dawn Star questioned the ways of the One, but this lay heavy on his mind.

He then heard words of the One spoken to him. Whether they were fresh words of the moment or an echo from the recent conversation, he couldn't be sure, but he heard them loud and clear nonetheless.

"Stay away from that tree."

The days after creation continued on in idyllic routine, which began with the Dawn Star singing in the morning. Every creature whose kingdom was the light of day awakened to the Dawn Star's song. To the those that ruled the night, it was like a lullaby that soothed them to sleep within the burrows, caves, hallows, or thickets where they rested during the daylight hours. In the evening, Gloria's songs from the stars quietly rained down from the heavens. The whole Earth was filled with song.

In the garden, Adam and Eve woke together, along with any animal that had happened to curl up next to them during the night. Often it was one or more of the great cats that purred alongside them or under them on any given day and stretched along with them as they greeted the morning and the Lord, who was waiting for them. After choosing and gathering what fruit to eat that day, they tended to the garden and animals as God had asked them to. They divided their daily routine in such a way that found Eve taking care of the animals and the man accepting the responsibility of growing more plants and trees.

Though it was work and sometimes arduous, the man and the woman maintained a consistent lightheartedness. The sound of their joy and laughter co-mingled with the songs of the garden.

In those early days and years, the music of creation was ever present upon the Earth and in the heavens. It was as if everything surrounding Adam and Eve were singing. It delighted the Dawn Star to hear the songs he had first brought to life from the tree of songs being echoed back to him from the very elements for which they were intended.

Every day for a time, the One was physically present with the beloved, teaching them about every aspect of Eden, including how best to prepare the soil and when it was time to start seeding and planting. He instructed them on what plants were best for certain animals and how to make sure they would have enough food in the future. Many of the animals in the garden they needed not to be concerned about, for they would forage for their own food, of which there was plenty in Eden … for all.

Part of their education involved sitting quietly with the One and watching the various behavior of birds and animals alike. They learned what plants, seeds, or grubs suited the individual species the best. They were also privy to the mating and birthing processes of all the creatures and came to understand the time and season in which it was to happen.

The Dawn Star, Gabriel, and Michael, as well of the rest of the host, were present at the birth of the first animal to be born in the garden after the completion of creation—a lamb and its twin. When the time for the birth grew close, the One moved quietly toward the mother and caught the first lamb as it came out from its mother's womb. He beckoned for the beloved to join Him, and He placed it in Eve's arm and indicated for Adam to catch its sibling. The Lord then directed them to lay their individual charges onto soft turf, where the creatures immediately struggled to their feet amid soft bleating. They discovered their mother's milk and fell silent as they began to suckle.

The Dawn Star and rest of the host of heaven marveled at what they were witnessing. All of heaven had witnessed every aspect of creation, from the first time light penetrated the darkness to the forming of the beloved from the clay of the Earth. What was first believed to be the end of creation, they now realized was merely the beginning of it and that the Lord had fashioned within it the ability for creation to replenish, renew, and recreate itself. It was at this moment that the Dawn Star came to realize the true meaning of the Lord's command to His creation: "Be fruitful and fill the Earth."

Adam and Eve lay on their stomachs, with their heads propped on their arms, watching the lambs take in nourishment from their mother. Directing his attention toward them, the Dawn Star wondered if that command applied to the woman and man as well. Would they be under the same compulsion as the rest of nature, to recreate themselves?

While the rest of the host seemed to rejoice at what was taking place, the Dawn Star found the moment strangely unsettling, especially as it pertained to the two humans. They had been given an integral role in the continuation of creation. These and every other living thing on Earth appeared to have been given something that he had not … the ability to give life.

THE SONG

After the initial introduction to the garden and the clarification of their responsibilities in caring for it, the beloved in time seemed to have moved from a teacher-pupil relationship with the One to one that was more collaborative in nature. The Dawn Star noticed Eve and Adam began to make plans for the garden without necessarily seeking the Lord's approval. In fact, He seemed very pleased with their changes and innovations to His original design. From the Dawn Star's point of view, this seemed presumptuous of the beloved, to change something that in his mind didn't need to be changed in the first place.

With the tools the Lord helped them create, they broke the garden's pristine turf to create rows for trees and plants to grow in when their seeds were sown. They dug into the clay found at the edge of the streams and made vessels to carry water and store grass and grain for the animals.

They learned to weave grass into vessels as well, into which they put the food they gathered for the day. The woman even went so far as to pick flowers from time to time and weave them into crowns that they wore on their heads. Images of the animals that wandered in and out of the garden appeared in mosaics on the ground, created with elements found in the garden. The touch of the man and the woman was becoming as prevalent upon the garden as that of the One.

When they were with the One, the beloved seemed to the Dawn Star to be getting far too familiar for his tastes. There was lots of hugging, teasing, and playing with the One … and incessant talking, far more than the Dawn Star felt was appropriate considering they were just humans. He enjoyed a similar familiarity with the Lord, but that was different; he was an archangel of the city of God … the first. From the Dawn Star's point of view, his position should carry with it privileges not shared by others.

There was something else the Dawn Star felt uneasy about. As he observed God's sweet and loving interactions with the man and the woman, he felt that it somehow diminished the relationship he had with the One, which up to this point he had thought special and unique. He didn't understand it.

It came to the point that the Dawn Star became critical of almost everything the beloved did and cast a sort of judgment upon them. He didn't think Adam and Eve treated the Lord and His garden with much reverence, and he felt God had given them far too much freedom to suit him.

The Dawn Star knew he had to come to terms with these thoughts and feelings, especially since he continued to always feel the presence of the Lord and the urgings of the Spirit to accept how things were with the beloved and accept them wholeheartedly as they were. The Dawn Star was being urged to love them. In his heart, this was something he was willing to do. Then he heard someone singing in the garden.

He heard it as he sat beneath the center cathedral opening of God's holy temple, overlooking all of creation.

The Dawn Star was intimately familiar with the singing voice of every member of his host. Upon one note, he could instantly identify who was singing. He had never heard this voice before. The garden, as well as all of creation, was filled with music. Each had their song of which he was equally familiar, but the Dawn Star did not know this song. He had never heard it before. He immediately left the temple and ventured into the garden in search of the mysterious tune.

The Lord had left the garden after the early morning, and the beloved were going about their daily routine. The Dawn Star soon discovered the song and its source when he found Adam digging into the soil. He was singing.

"My Father is the Lord of all creation,
and I give Him all my love.
This garden is His, which He gave to us,
the water, the earth, and the sky above.
Thank you, Father. Thank you, Father,
for all the stars and trees.
Thank you, Father. Thank you, Father,
for making all of these.
My Father is the Lord of all creation,
and I give Him all my love."

The Dawn Star had never heard this song before, much less had sung it. It was completely foreign to him. He knew every song in creation but was ignorant of this tune, which made him feel unsettled in his spirit.

As he worked, Adam sang the song over and over without seeming to think about it at all, like it was a natural part of who he was. Eve, who was a short distance away, tending to the needs of some of the animals, began to sing the tune along with him in the same easy manner. At one point, she broke into a simple harmony. Their two voices became one voice. That one song became their song.

The Dawn Star, who seemed to always know what to do and what to say, was motionless and speechless. Before, it had always been second nature for him to join his voice to a song being sung. At this point, with this song, he was silent. When they had completed their work, Adam and Eve walked away hand in hand to another part of the garden, still singing the new song.

He still heard the song as he ascended back to God's holy temple in search for the answer regarding the mystery and origin of it. He passed through the temple, down the golden staircase, and through the palace of all things to the source of all songs, his tree.

As he walked through the open amethyst doors, any uneasiness he was feeling about what he had heard in the garden seemed to drift away. A quiet peace took its place as he gazed up at the tree of songs. The Dawn Star was confident he would find the answers he was looking for in the branches and among the light fruit that grew upon them.

He glided up to the top of the tree to begin his search. What he was looking for, he didn't know exactly. Something different, something out of place, perhaps a light fruit he had overlooked.

The tree was as full of fruit as when the Dawn Star had first encountered it. After he and his host absorbed the songs contained within them, another fruit of the same song grew in its place to be stored there for as long as necessary. The Dawn Star knew the song contained within each fruit by just looking at it and by where it was located on the tree. If there was something out of the ordinary, he would know it.

As the Dawn Star descended through branches, he took note of all the fruit on all the branches and smiled to himself as he relived in his mind each moment of joyful discovery for each song when it was given birth by his voice. When he drew nearer to the bottom, he was no closer to knowing the origin of the man's song, but he was no longer troubled in his spirit. The tree of songs was just as he had left it, just as it should be. He would speak with the One regarding the song's origin, and the Lord would put to rest any unease he felt about it. In comparison to what grew in the branches of his beloved tree, the song of the man was a very little thing and not worth being concerned about.

His feet touched the floor of the palace, and he made to leave the chamber. But when he happened to look up, on a low hanging limb he observed a speck of light appearing at the end of a thin branch. It began to grow larger until it reached a diameter of about three inches, where it seemed to settle in as if it belonged with the rest of the light fruit in the tree. A new song joining all the other songs around it.

The appearance of the new light fruit took the Dawn Star by surprise. For a long time, he simply stared up at it. He knew by the look of it, it was no song he had encountered before. The branch it grew upon held no previous occupant. It was like the limb had grown there specifically to hold this new arrival. His mind raced with questions: *Where did it come from? What song does it hold? Why has it now appeared?*

The unease that had left his spirit when he arrived at the tree suddenly returned when he thought of an answer. This was the song in the garden, growing on the tree of songs, his tree. He stood unmoving as he let this revelation settle upon him. He looked at the fruit and couldn't bring himself to touch it much less absorb it … and sing it. Not this song. He had seen what happened when the songs from the tree were sung; they took on a life of their own. They were woven into the fabric of creation. He couldn't with this song. He couldn't allow it. He felt that it would somehow diminish all the glorious songs that grew there if he were to lend his voice to it. It didn't belong on his tree.

He looked up at the small glowing fruit and then turned and walked through the doors, feeling as if some light had gone out of him, feeling like his beloved tree of songs had somehow disappointed him, let him down … even betrayed him a little.

The Dawn Star turned his back on the tree in search of the One, who would give him the answers he so desperately needed … or so he hoped.

A CONFRONTATION

The Dawn Star came upon the One sitting on a rocky promontory on the edge of the western ocean. As he approached, he observed the One reach across from His right to His left and then quickly extend his hand out from Him, flinging out in a large cluster of tiny bits of his glory.

Out from the shore, gathering above the ocean, a great noisy crowd of sea birds dove and snatched the bits of glory in their beaks before they fell into the water. The bits that escaped the birds and made it to the water were quickly consumed by boiling schools of fish gathered near the surface. The One stood and, with a deep left-to-right thrust of His hand, released another cluster of glory to another part of the ocean just as a great leviathan breached the surface in time to swallow it all in its large, outstretched open maw.

At this sight, the One laughed in delight. He clapped enthusiastically as the leviathan settled back into the water with a thunderous foamy splash.

The Dawn Star often marveled at the One's astonishment and

wonder of His own creation. The One who designed a million flowers down to the last detail, selected the colors they would wear, created the process in which they grew, live, reproduce, and thrive seemed to always be in constant awe of what His hands had created. Even now as the sea and its creatures danced before Him, they had an appreciative audience in the Person of their Creator.

With the One still looking out at the sea, the Dawn Star spoke to Him.

"The man sang a song in the garden today that I didn't know."

The One smiled and said, "Yes, he did."

"Where did it come from?" the Dawn Star asked. "It didn't grow from the tree of songs until recently, because I knew all the songs that grow there."

"The song came from him," replied the One.

"Did you give it to him?"

"No. The song was all his. I knew it was there. I designed within him the ability to create it. What did you think of the man's song?"

The Dawn Star stood quietly as he took in this new information. After a moment, he replied, "It wasn't perfect. The notes were inconsistent, his voice cracked in places, some of the words seemed forced to fit the melody. It was far too simple for my taste. Like I said, it wasn't perfect."

"Did it need to be?" the One asked.

"Every song that is sung by Your creation is perfect. Every song that grows in the tree of songs is perfect. My host and I sing them perfectly. Your creation is perfect. Your city is perfect. You are perfect. This man created by Your hand should be perfect. Therefore, what comes from him should be perfect as well."

"I thought it was perfect," the One said.

"Lord, it was full of mistakes."

"I didn't notice any mistakes. Opportunities for growth, perhaps, but no mistakes. Did you really listen to the song?" the One asked.

"I did. That's why I knew it wasn't perfect."

"Is that all you paid attention to? The imperfections?"

"In a perfect world, it is not that difficult to notice the mistakes."

"The man was singing to Me," said the One. "It is a song about the garden I put him in. It is about the beauty of the flowers, trees, and creatures that I have surrounded him and the woman with. But more, it was a hymn of appreciation and love to Me for what I have done. It came from the truth of his heart, pure, clean, and innocent … and that's what made it perfect."

"Mistakes and all?" the Dawn Star asked.

"Yes," answered the One. "Even with the mistakes you heard, it was perfect. Mistakes are a tool by which the beloved can learn. They are steps they take that allow opportunities for them to be taught by Me. Every lesson leads them to a greater discovery of who I am and who I created, and designed them to be. The man and woman are my beloved children, created in my perfect love. Therefore, they are perfect … as they are.

The One paused and then said, "I look forward to hearing the next song they sing."

They both were quiet as the sounds of birds and crashing surf accompanied their silence. The One resumed feeding the sea with His glory. The Dawn Star let the last words of the One settle on him until a troubling thought came into his mind, which he expressed in a question to the Lord.

"There will be more?"

"Oh yes," said the One. "Many more, and not just songs, but music of all forms and variations, and works of art, and architecture. There will be books and stories, written words turned into poetry, and scientific achievements. When they are ready, they will move beyond the boundaries of the garden. They will bring forth from the Earth all manner of crops and vegetation. They will bear children and populate the ends of the Earth. They will build cities and communities whose beauty will only be rivaled by my own city. The beloved will dwell together in peace, praise, and love. I will walk among them all … and what wonders we will create together."

The Dawn Star asked, "How can this be? You speak of the beloved as if they were the very reflection of your glory, as will be the achievements You say they will accomplish."

"Exactly!" exclaimed the One.

The Dawn Star continued, "But, I saw … all of heaven saw how they were made. You knelt, put your hands in the dust of the ground, took a lump of earth, and pushed and formed this lump into what he is now. Without your breath inside him, that is all he, they will be … nothing but an elaborate form of dust."

The One spoke quietly after a moment. "The beloved are far from dust, and you know that."

The Dawn Star remembered the violet firmament at the top of the great hall, with the tiny, swirling, laughing, singing points of light. He then remembered the unending song of the beloved, which he had sung with the One there. The simple figures that lived in the garden did not measure up to the level of emotion expressed in the song. To the Dawn Star, they did not seem worthy of the love and expectation the song expressed.

"I do not share your opinion of them."

The One said, "Thoughts and opinions are yours to have. It is how I created you. It is the way you can love and serve Me with your whole heart. It is enough that I love the beloved as I do … as deeply as I do."

"Can you explain this love to me?" the Dawn Star asked. "Because

I do not understand it. Love for the stars, galaxies, and nebulae for their sheer size, color, majesty, and songs they bring to the universe … the green of the earth and majesty of the mountains, trees swaying in praise, flowers bursting with color, the grass on the plains and savannas bending to and fro as the great and gentle winds dance with it in the light of the day, and this"—he turns to the western sea roiling with life, sound, and movement—"for all its power and vibrant mystery … and all the creatures made by your hand … the flyers, the swimmers, the runners, the walkers, and the crawlers … love for these I understand. But not for the ones who stumble around your perfect garden without a care or purpose, barely mindful of anything around them."

The One stood and looked into the golden eyes of the Dawn Star. "There exists in Me that which is unexplainable … no language to describe it … no tool with which to measure it … no word to define it … no power to change it … no formula to calculate it. That is My love for the beloved. It has always been as I have been. All I ask is that you serve them as you love and serve Me."

The Dawn Star remembered the first time he sat in the branches of the tree of songs with the One when He gifted him with the tree and the awesome responsibility of leading His host. It had been his great joy to accept and lead them as the heavenly chorus for the glory of the One. He loved his host. They were a beautiful, bright, and wondrous sight, especially when they sang.

But now, the One was speaking of an additional responsibility, a responsibility of service to beings who reflected more of the dust of the Earth than the glory of God. He was the Dawn Star, master of songs, leader of angels, and servant only to the One. To accomplish what the One was asking was not something he could easily comprehend.

In serving the beloved, he wouldn't know where to begin. The One answered the Dawn Star's unspoken question.

"Inspire them. I made you for that purpose. You are an inspiration to your brother archangels, to your host, and to all of heaven. You were the first to sing all the songs of creation. No one knew the song of trees until you sang it or that of the sparrow, leviathan, or dolphin. You were the first to sing the song of the beloved. Your star is the last light of night. It shines to proclaim the promise of a bright new day. You shine bright for them, the way to glorify and praise My name. You will show them how to strive to be excellent in all their ways."

The Dawn Star thought about what the One was saying and what that would imply.

"To do what You are asking, it would mean that I would be among them. I would be known to them," he said.

"Only as I will it to be. Everything will come from Me. But yes, in the fullness of time You will be revealed to them as all in my kingdom will be revealed to them eventually. It is My desire to share everything with them."

"Everything?" the Dawn Star asked.

"Yes," the One replied. "Everything I have is theirs. That is the depth of My love for them. I do not hold the Earth back from them. They have dominion over all that I have created. Heaven will not be kept from them. The very best of who I am is for them … As they walk with Me in My ways, I will give them ways to walk in. It is My desire to have them with Me … always. And I with them."

As the Dawn Star took in the words of the One, an uneasy feeling smoldered within him. The truth was he didn't want to be around them. He wanted very little to do with them now. The words "they are not worthy" thundered in his mind with every declaration the One spoke about them. They were, in the Dawn Star's estimation, barely worthy of the life they'd been given, let alone dominion over all creation. To hold the eventual promise of heaven for them was even more unthinkable.

But there was more eating at the Dawn Star's spirit. Evidently, they had been given the ability to create, a gift that had been denied him and the rest of the host. He and the host could sing and proclaim the beauty and glory of what was already created but without creating it themselves. To the Dawn Star, the act of creation meant making something out of nothing, like the One bringing forth from the nothingness of the waters the earth, the skies, the seas, and all that dwelled within them, as well as the planets, the stars, and the galaxies spinning in the universe.

Though the man's song was simple in its form and execution, it had come from him. It wasn't grown on a tree or presented to him as a gift. It was his alone. It was nothing until the man made it something. He created it.

The Dawn Star had great appreciation, curiosity, and wonder about that which his senses could experience around him, perhaps even more than any of the other heavenly beings. But he could not sing a song that did not already exist. He could not put together words and music of his own to make one. He had to rely completely on what was given to him by God or the tree.

The Dawn Star could not create. But the creatures from the dust could. They had a piece of what had belonged utterly and completely to God. The creative was what made the One God. From the nothingness of the waters came forth all of creation. It was not adapted, conceived, borrowed, or inspired from anything else. It was all from God and God alone, and that ability to create was also in the hands of the woman and the man.

The Dawn Star said, "They can create."

"Yes," said the One.

"You can create … You made them … like you," said the Dawn Star.

"Not like me. They are created in My image, yes. They are exactly as I have willed and designed them to be. I have given them gifts that no other creature on Earth or in heaven possess. They have the ability and desire to draw unto Me and be with Me, and I desire to be with them … But they are not like Me. I am uncreated. I have always been and will always be. There is no one like Me."

The Dawn Star understood and heard some of what the One was saying, but a single thought kept the attention of his mind more than the One's words: *the beloved can create and I cannot.* This thought created a feeling in him that he had never felt before. It was a strange and intrusive feeling, directed at his thoughts of the beloved. They had something the Dawn Star would never have.

There was much that, as an archangel, the Dawn Star could accomplish that others of the heavenly host could not. His was the lead voice of the songs of creation. He was the one who taught heaven and Earth how to sing them. Outside of the One, it was his voice most heard in creation … yet the melodies he sang were not his own. The Dawn Star did not create them. He had no knowledge of how to begin an original tune, much less how to place words into it to fit a tune. The Dawn Star could only duplicate what he was shown or what he heard. He could recognize beauty, but he could not create it. Moreover, as he was critical of the man's original song, pointing out its every flaw and imperfection, he had no knowledge of how to correct the flaws and make it perfect in his eyes. He only recognized what it was lacking.

He could not put into words the feelings invading his spirit like a dark shadow, crowding out the beauty that surrounded him even to the point it affected how he reacted to the glory of the One. The beloved had been given a gift that he did not have, one that in his opinion they did not deserve. The Dawn Star realized that he had been given much in his position as an archangel—his beloved tree of songs, his host, the brotherhood and friendship of Michael and Gabriel, citizenship in the kingdom of heaven, and complete access to God and His glory. But within the darkness slowly gripping his heart, there was the knowledge that everything he had was all the Dawn Star would ever have.

His thoughts were interrupted by the voice of the One as He looked out to the western sea. "No one can sing like you do."

The Dawn Star, in mild surprise, looked at the One.

"In all creation, there is no voice more beautiful or perfect than yours. When you sing, you are the bringer of much light and joy. You have been given so many gifts already. You have been a witness to every aspect of creation, even your own. You witnessed the birth of your brothers. You were there when the heavenly host came into being. You have been given more than anyone will ever have."

The Dawn Star looked at the Lord and said, "But I can't create."

"I created you as a frame for creation. To enhance it, to call attention to it with how you sing. The sun will rise every morning whether you sing it in or not, but when you do …" The One paused for a moment and closed his eyes, living some unseen moment of His own. "But when you sing, a new hope, a new glory, is added to what is already beautiful and perfect and full of promise … You make it better."

The Dawn Star was taken aback by the words of the One to him. At that moment, he felt a greater sense of God's love for him and perhaps even His admiration. But that couldn't be. The One had no need to admire anything except the work of his own hands. How could the Dawn Star make something better just by singing?

"I just sing the songs that were given to me through the tree of songs. They are Your songs, not mine," he said.

"And you sing them like no other," said the One.

"But I didn't create them. You did. They are not my songs!"

"When you sing them, they might as well be. You, my dear Dawn Star, have the most beautiful voice in the universe. That is my greatest gift to you. No one is like you … No one can sing like you do. No one."

Again, he had the feeling of God's admiration, the awareness of His love. For this moment, it should have been enough, but it wasn't. The questions simmering at his spirit remained.

"Why can't I create? Why do they have a part of You that I don't?"

"Because it is a gift I have given to them."

"I want that gift," said the Dawn Star quietly.

"It is their gift, not yours. You have gifts they will never have … can't have. Because they're your gifts. It is how I want it to be. It is how I have willed it to be. Let it be enough."

The Dawn Star persisted. "I want it. I want what they have. Why can't You give it to me?"

The voice of the One became harder. "The gift has been given. It will not be taken back. It belongs to them and no other."

The words of the One lay heavy upon the Dawn Star's heart. He stood unmoving at the edge of the cliff. He tried to brush away the thoughts of the beloved having what he did not and would not. He tried to focus on the love the One had for him and the abundance of the gifts God had given him. He desperately wanted it to be enough … but it wasn't. He wanted more.

Suddenly, he felt the presence of the One upon him. His love engulfed him. He smiled and closed his eyes to receive it. The familiar, pleasing warmth of the One filled him, and he began to sense the release of his troubling thoughts concerning the beloved. He felt their shadow vacating his spirit and the light of God's love for him bringing peace and contentment.

He did not know how long they stood there together with the great ocean roaring beneath them, and it didn't matter. To the Dawn Star, he might as well have been back at the temple where it all began or standing beneath the tree of songs for the first time or in all the times he had been so abundantly aware of God's love for him. In this moment, it was just the Dawn Star and the One. Nothing else existed to him right now … not the beloved, not his host, not Gloria, not even Michael and Gabriel. It was just him and the One. No one else. The One's voice broke through the stillness.

"I love them, the beloved, as I love you … I ask you to love them as I do."

The moment with the One was broken. The shadow around his heart that had receded came creeping back, wrapping its tendrils around any affection for the beloved the Dawn Star might have had and chasing it away.

For the first time since he came to life in the temple, the Dawn Star walked away from the One and took to the sky. As he hovered above, he looked down upon the Lord and said, "If You love me as You love them, give me that part of You that You gave them."

When no answer was forthcoming from the One, the Dawn Star returned in silence to the city of God and left the Lord standing on the rocky cliff beside the western ocean.

25

A GATHERING OF ANGELS

After his conversation with the One on the shore of the western ocean, the Dawn Star kept to himself. He took his post in creation every morning to sing in the dawn without fail. Then he retreated back to the glass tabernacle of praise. After all, that task still belonged to him.

As the rest of the heavenly host occupied themselves with the duties of heaven and Earth, the Dawn Star brooded alone in the place that was made for him. He had no desire to venture out into the city of God knowing it would eventually have to be shared with the creatures of the dust, as he now referred to the beloved in his mind. But this place he would not share with them. They would never enter this place. He would sing the doors closed and shut them out if necessary.

He stared at the golden vista outside the glass walls of the cathedral. His finger traced the path of a crack that he remembered had appeared right after he returned from his confrontation with the One.

On that day, when he'd made his way back to heaven and to the tabernacle, Gloria, Allegro, and several other members of his host had been there singing together in a group. He paid no mind to what they were singing but simply said to them, "I wish to be alone."

"Come sing with us," several said, waving their indication for him to join them.

"Leave me," he said with an edge to his voice they had not heard before.

Taken back by his tone, the group rose slowly and filed out in silence. As Gloria passed by the Dawn Star, she stopped and touched his hand. He looked down at her blankly, and she stared back at him intently as if to discover some hidden mystery and meaning in his actions.

After a moment, he simply repeated, "Leave me."

Gloria let go of his hand and left him standing alone just inside the threshold of the tabernacle. Without moving, he sang the doors closed behind her.

The Dawn Star was alone for the first time in his life. In that moment, he had effectively cut himself off from everything and everyone that had shaped his existence and purpose. He was alone, but his spirit felt crowded with strange and new feelings brought on by his conversation with the One and the song the man had sung in the garden.

It was the man's song and his alone. He made it up, so to speak. He, the Dawn Star, the singer of all songs, the one who taught heaven and Earth how to sing, the greatest voice in the universe according to the One … had nothing to do with it. It had been created and sung apart from him.

The Man created it. Those words kept ringing in his mind. *The man created it. The man created it ... he created it ... he created it ... he created it ... he created ... the man created ...*

With that final unrelenting thought, the feelings roiling up within him could be contained no longer. They came out at once, but not in a controlled, orderly fashion as it was when he sang. This was an explosion of out-of-control emotion. It was just sound … no discernible tune or words. It was loud, and it seemed to come from his very soul, from an unexplainable, unidentifiable hurt. He was screaming. He was positioned above the floor in the center of the cathedral, and the sound echoed back and forth off the walls. With the doors closed, no one in heaven heard him scream. He was completely alone and cut off.

After the echo of the Dawn Star's scream faded into silence, the sound of a single crack appearing on the wall was the only thing heard before it was quiet again.

He didn't know how long he was alone in the glass cathedral. There was no sense of the passing of time there. It was measured only by the frequency of how many times the Dawn Star sang in the morning, even while he kept to himself there. He never counted. He just sang because that's what he did.

He had spoken to no one outside of his host since he last spoke to the One. He could hear his brothers, Michael and Gabriel, calling for him from time to time. He would see them outside the glass cathedral wall, searching for him, but he made no effort to sing the doors open to allow them inside. Even though he opened them to sing in the dawn and his brothers were there waiting for him, he would brush past them without so much as a look or a word.

He could give no reason for his self-isolation except for his feelings that centered around the humans in the garden. He couldn't bear to refer to them as the beloved anymore, for that was the farthest from what they were to the Dawn Star. He had no love for them. He didn't know what it was, but it wasn't love, at least not how the One described His love for them—unexplainable, indescribable, unmeasurable, undefinable, unchanging. What he felt for them was anything but that, and what's more, he didn't want to feel that way for them.

He knew he was alone in his opinion of them. No one in heaven felt as he did. To the host, even his brothers, they were the beloved and would always be. They would not accept the truth about them, that they were creatures of the dust and would always be so to the Dawn Star. They had been given a gift they did not deserve. They weren't worthy of it. They were not worthy of any of the gifts they were given or would be given, including heaven.

Heaven, the city of God and angels, the Dawn Star's home. In his mind, it was the best of everything created by the One, greater than the Earth and all the cosmos. The moment he had opened his eyes and taken his first breath, he had known this was where he belonged. The more he allowed his brooding to linger on the idea that heaven would also belong to the humans in time, the more an idea cemented itself into his spirit, an idea best described in one word, *no.*

This cannot happen. It must not happen, he thought to himself. *I cannot let this happen.* There was a shift in his thoughts, and he spoke them to himself aloud: "We can't let this happen." It occurred to him that perhaps the rest of the host was not aware of the One's plans to share heaven with the man and the woman and those like them.

They must be told., he thought. *They must be made aware that their city will no longer just belong to them. It will belong to creatures of the dust. No! This must not happen.*

He resolved that he would begin dispensing this information to his own host first. Surely there were others in the Dawn Star's company who would agree with his sentiments regarding humans. There must be others who would find the notion of sharing heaven with the creatures of the Earth as appalling and repugnant as himself. If there weren't, he would convince them and win them over to his way of thinking. They must see that the plans the One had for His "beloved" were foolish. The city of God belonged to the host of heaven and them alone.

"Let them have the Earth. Heaven is ours and ours alone, and we will not share what belongs to us," he said to himself. "If we cannot share or have what has been given to them, then we will not share heaven with them. This is what must be said."

After the Dawn Star sang in the morning one day, he did not return immediately to the tabernacle of praise, which was his custom of late. Instead, he ventured into the palace of all things and went directly to his tree of songs with the intention of gathering his host together in the tabernacle.

He found two of his host at the base of the tree, Adagio and Sonata, singing a duet together. Though it was beautiful and soothing to hear, the Dawn Star barely acknowledged it.

He said to them abruptly, "Gather our host to the cathedral without delay."

Although the duo was taken aback by the terse nature of the command, they simply nodded in an affirmative motion. The Dawn Star turned quickly away to return to the tabernacle of praise and await his host.

"Brother!" came a shout from across the great hall, followed by the massive bronze arms of Michael engulfing him from behind.

"I have missed you … We have missed you!" he said as he jostled the Dawn Star up and down and turned him around. "What have you been doing closed up in that glass bubble of yours?"

Trying to control his irritation, the Dawn Star said, "Put me down, Michael!" Despite his best efforts, it still came across as if he were scolding a child.

The big archangel stopped the movement and slowly set the

golden angel onto the floor. Michael's broad grin disappeared and was replaced by a look of bewilderment. The Dawn Star had never spoken to him or anyone like that before. What was more to the point, the Dawn Star had always referred to him as "brother." He usually never used his name when addressing him.

They both became aware that the palace had grown completely silent because of the exchange. The angels present in the great hall had stopped whatever they were doing and were now staring at the Dawn Star. Gabriel came out of the room of God's word and was standing in the threshold when he caught the Dawn Star's eye. The three archangels exchanged glances until the Dawn Star turned to leave through the jade doors. No other words were spoken.

As he exited the palace, the Dawn Star looked up to the top of the golden staircase and saw the One standing there, surrounded by His glory. It was the first time he had seen the Lord since the confrontation on the rocky cliff by the sea. Before, upon seeing the One, he would have walked, run, or flown up the stairs as quickly as possible just to be with Him. Instead, he turned and made his way back to the glass tabernacle, and the One let him go.

The host of the Dawn Star made their way to the tabernacle of praise, having received the message from Adagio and Sonata. On any other occasion, it would have been a joyful, uplifting journey, but upon hearing of the encounter between the Dawn Star and Michael, which had been witnessed by some of his host, the mood was more somber than usual.

The doors of the tabernacle were wide open, which hadn't been the case for some time. The host began to make their way inside. Gloria and Allegro, who were traveling together, saw the Spirit standing outside and opposite the open doors. The soft jewel-toned glory of the

Spirit always seemed to add a sweet nature to the overall character of the One.

Gloria looked at the Spirit and then the open door. "Are You coming in?"

The Spirit looked down at the small angel and smiled. "No. I haven't been invited."

"Is that necessary? Can't You go in and out wherever You want to?"

"Yes. But it's best to be invited."

"Well, come with us then," said Gloria, looking at Allegro and then back to the Spirit. "I will invite you."

"This isn't your invitation to give. It doesn't belong to you. It belongs to the Dawn Star," the Spirit said, nodding toward the open doors.

"So You are not going inside with us?"

"No, little one," the Spirit said. "I don't think he wants me there, the Dawn Star."

Gloria stood still and looked toward the inside of the tabernacle as the rest of the host filed in. Allegro made to follow them when Gloria took his hand and said, "Wait, Allegro."

He stopped.

"I'm staying out here with the Spirit. who hasn't been invited to come inside. If the Spirit can't go in, I don't want to go in." At that, she took her place beside the Spirit.

Allegro looked at the open doors and then back at Gloria and the Spirit, seeming conflicted in his own spirit. Among the host of the Dawn Star, Allegro showed the greatest devotion toward him. Everything he was asked to do he did with exuberance and joy. He loved singing with the host of heaven and singing the songs of creation with the Dawn Star. He also loved and adored Gloria and appreciated her quiet leadership among the host and, of course, her gift in singing.

Though nothing could compare to the singing voice of the Dawn Star overall, Gloria's was a close second.

He stood looking into the ebony eyes of his tiny friend when he heard the voice of the Dawn Star from inside the glass tabernacle. He turned and saw that he was elevated off the floor in the center of the room, at the same level with the open doors. His body shone with a golden light.

"Dear ones," said the Dawn Star. "In a few moments I will share with you, news that will change heaven forever."

Murmurings and questions were heard among the group. A voice near Allegro spoke aloud. It was Sonata.

"What is it, my lord?"

Allegro turned and looked at them, suddenly remembering the time when he had inadvertently referred to the Dawn Star as lord and was immediately corrected and told in no uncertain terms that the One was Lord and no one else. He waited for the correction to come from the Dawn Star. None came.

"In time you will know all things," was all he said.

It was then that a decision was made. Allegro stepped back away from the entrance and took his place beside the Spirit, his one true Lord. The rest of the host remained inside the cathedral, waiting for what would come next from the Dawn Star.

From his elevated position, the Dawn Star could see the Spirit, Gloria, and Allegro standing together outside the cathedral. When the last of the host took their places within the large glass room, he prepared in his mind to sing the doors closed but was aware of the Spirit looking directly at him. Then it was no longer just the Spirit but the complete fullness of the One standing at a distance before him.

For the first time in his life, he felt the distance from God as if it were a physical thing, a barrier that seemed to separate them from one another. This feeling was foreign to the Dawn Star. Perhaps the separation he now felt had begun casting a shadow around his heart after the confrontation on the western shore, growing more prevalent the longer he had remained isolated from the rest of heaven in his tabernacle.

There was a moment as he was looking into the face of the One that the Dawn Star longed to be restored into full fellowship with Him, to experience the joy of being with the Lord without conditions and reservations … before the cliff, before the man's song, even before he had witnessed his formation from the dust. When it was just God, His city, the heavenly host, and himself, the Dawn Star … before he was fully aware of the One's plans for his "beloved" and all they had been given.

Perhaps he would have liked to remain blissfully ignorant of all of this, and he would have if it weren't for the song from the man that he could hear echoing in his mind and heart, reminding him of what he did not have and would never have. It was gift for humans alone … God had made that perfectly clear to him.

Just before the last shadows of his heart separated him completely from God, he heard the faint words of the One in his head, *Don't do this. Just love them.* It was too late. The separation was complete.

The Dawn Star opened his mouth and sang the doors of the tabernacle of praise closed, leaving the One and two of his own host outside. In a short while, the light of the glory of God, which always indicated the presence of the One, was no longer visible through the glass walls. The Dawn Star and his host were completely alone inside the tabernacle.

All eyes were directed to him. Everything was still and quiet. The Dawn Star turned slowly around, looking at each of them. One of the host evidently uncomfortable with the stillness and lack of activity, spoke out a question.

"What are we going to sing?"

The Dawn Star snapped his head in the direction of the speaker and stared, startling them. "After hearing what I have to tell you, we might never raise our voices in song in heaven again."

The host began to question and murmur among themselves. "What does this mean?" they asked each other.

The Dawn Star observed the surprise and shock taking hold of them and registering on their faces. He let them continue to feel agitated and uncomfortable for quite some time. Then he raised his hands with the intention of settling them. Slowly their voices died down, and their attention was turned completely again upon the Dawn Star.

"My dear host!" he said. "Heaven is our home, and we are the host of heaven!"

They all spoke in affirmation and agreement with what the Dawn Star had declared.

"In this place, we sing all the songs of heaven and Earth. They are all our songs, given to us by the tree of songs. We taught the entirety of the host of heaven to sing them. We sang them first!" The Dawn Star's voice began rise in intensity and came to a crescendo as he said, "Heaven is filled with song because of us!"

Caught up in the moment, the entire host began to shout and cheer in agreement: "Yes!"

"But, my dear host, this will not always be so. Changes are coming to heaven. The songs of heaven will not be just ours anymore. Other voices will join the songs of angels."

At this point, the host had become completely quiet. The Dawn Star understood at this point that he had their complete attention.

As every eye watched, he rose to the top of the domed roof of his tabernacle.

He continued, "Their songs will co-mingle with ours. Heaven will be tainted by them, it,s glory diminished. In time, the heaven we know …" He paused as he watched the intended effect of his words register on each face. " …will be no more!"

A collective sound of exclamation and shock rose from the host, along with questions.

"How can this be?"

"Whose songs?"

"What changes?"

The Dawn Star allowed them to continue to question and express their astonishment over this revelation. From his vantage point, he observed the confusion it was causing among the ranks of his host. For some reason, he was strangely gratified by it all.

The noise in the tabernacle continued until a single question rose above it all.

"Lord Dawn Star, what will be the cause of these changes in heaven?"

The Dawn Star looked down upon them all as the room grew silent to hear the answer. A slight smile came across his face as he responded with an edge of contempt in his voice.

"The beloved!"

At his words, a crack in the glass walls began to appear and made its way to the top of the dome. The Dawn Star did not know the reason for its sudden appearance, but the sound and image of it seemed to add a dramatic emphasis to his words. For whatever reason, the Dawn Star was gratified by the effect it had on his host.

Another collective gasp of astonishment filled the room, followed by more confusion.

From the midst of this, a voice shouted, "Does God know? The One must be told!"

There were shouts of agreement from all around the room. Again, the Dawn Star raised his hand to call them to silence. When they were still, he answered, "Yes. The Lord knows."

"What will He do about the changes in heaven?"

"Nothing," the Dawn Star replied simply. "He will do nothing … because eventually He will allow the humans to join us in heaven … It was His plan all along."

More shock and confusion.

Another voice spoke out. "If it is the One's will, then isn't a good plan? After all, everything the One decides and does is good. Isn't His creation and heaven itself proof of that?"

Others nodded and spoke in agreement with the statement.

The Dawn Star was taken aback by this logic. He had not anticipated this reasoning. In his mind, he could agree with this statement about the ultimate goodness of the One, but acknowledging this to his host would defeat his ultimate purpose. It would mean that he would have to accept that it—the fact that the man and the woman had been given a gift, the ability to create, that he did not possess because the One would not give it to him—was good.

He was not concerned whether others among the host were given this ability. In fact, if truth be told, the Dawn Star only wanted it for himself. If he couldn't have it, then no one else should either, especially the beloved. As far as he was concerned, this gift of creation should have been given to him in the first place. He felt as if the human creation had stolen it from him, which made the notion of eventually sharing heaven with them an idea that he could not, and would not, accept. The goal of the moment was to keep them out, and winning his host over was key to that goal.

"Yes. Indeed, everything the One has done is good, wonderful in fact," the Dawn Star declared. "It is all perfect. Perfection is what makes all this work." He waved his hands wide. "It is what makes the One God."

He continued, as he was sure he had all their attention.

"His creation is perfect. You who are a part of the host of heaven are perfect. I know this because I was there when the Lord God formed you all from His glory. I saw how He made all of us from that which is the One. We all have a piece of God, for we were made from Him. Therefore, we are perfect!"

A cheer rose up from the crowd at the Dawn Star's words. "Yes!"

"You, my host, are perfect."

"Yes!"

"All of heaven is perfect!"

"Yes!"

The affirmation of the crowd of angels echoed off the walls of the tabernacle. The Dawn Star was delighted by their raucous enthusiasm, for it was what he had intended from the beginning. They were united in this idea. After the noise faded away, the Dawn Star spoke again.

"But …" The word snapped from his lips in a crisp, joyless tone. "Will heaven retain its perfection when God allows the beloved to be with us here? What will become of the city of God then?"

The Dawn Star's questions subdued the crowd. They spoke quietly to one another in confusion. He could see the anxiety slowly creep upon each of them.

The Dawn Star continued, "We have seen what they have done to the garden God put them in. They walk around in it with no regard to its beauty. They create their own images out of the rocks and flowers. They dig in the ground and plant seeds in an attempt to make their own mark upon the garden. The One is allowing them to make the garden, and eventually all the Earth, their own. What do you think will happen to our home when they are allowed to enter heaven? Just like the garden, it will be marked, defaced, and changed by their influence. Mark my words."

All present in the vast tabernacle were silent as the Dawn Star spoke. All that could be heard was the occasional faint sound of cracks making their way across the crystal walls. The sound went all but unnoticed by those present. The Dawn Star's voice was all they seemed to hear.

"Did you hear that song in the garden? The one the man sang?"

The host spoke in questions among themselves. They seemed confused until one spoke up and said, "We all heard it."

"We thought it was one of ours," said another.

"It was not!" the Dawn Star said with greater volume.

They were silent again for a moment. Then the questions came.

"Where did it come from?"

"Did he get it from the tree of songs?"

"How did he obtain it?"

"Who gave it to him?"

After all the questions were spoken, the Dawn Star answered.

"The song came from him. He made it up."

They all stared at the Dawn Star blankly with no evidence of comprehension registering on their faces.

"The human created it," clarified the Dawn Star.

"I thought all music came from tree of songs," declared one angel.

"How can this be? Only God can create," said another.

The Dawn Star smiled in silent satisfaction and said, "Yes! Only God can create! This creature took something away from the One that should only belong to the Lord!"

The host erupted in shouts and noise.

The Dawn Star spoke above them. “If they will take this from God, what is to stop them from taking what was given to us? What’s to stop them from taking all of heaven for themselves! The heaven we know will be no more. Our songs will no longer be sung in the city of God!”

The clamor in response from the host was so loud, no one was aware of the sound of more cracks or their appearance up and across the crystal walls.

“Heaven, the city of God, must be safeguarded from the invasion of humanity!”

Another shout of affirmation came from those gathered.

“How can the One let this happen?” questioned one of the host.

The crowd grew quiet so they could hear the answer.

The Dawn Star looked at them and said, “Because He loves them, so He says.”

Another question came in an uncertain voice. “More than us?”

Until this moment, that concept had not occurred to the Dawn Star regarding the One. The idea of the Lord’s love being quantitative more to one than another was an alien thought to him. But considering what the beloved had been given that he was not, he concluded it was not out of the realm of possibility.

“It would seem so,” he said, speaking the lie without emotion. “And He wants us—no, He demands that we love them as well.”

“This cannot be!” a cry came from the host.

“It’s true!” said the Dawn Star. “He told me this Himself. The creatures of the dust will be given everything. They have the Earth. Their songs, their actions will mar the face of creation itself … What they do on Earth they will do in heaven when they arrive. And the One will let it happen!”

The cracks in the walls now came more frequently as the Dawn Star's lies progressed.

The shouts from the host reached their loudest point.

"No! No! No! We can't let it happen!"

As the Dawn Star looked upon the faces of his host, he saw an emotion he hadn't seen before. It was foreign to him. It was what was left when all joy and hope were stripped away and there was nothing left to hold on to. It was fear, and he was strangely gratified by what he saw happening to them.

"God can't let that happen!" they shouted collectively "The One must be stopped from doing this thing. We must stop Him!"

The Dawn Star smiled to himself in satisfaction. He had succeeded in convincing them.

"We will," he said.

"How?" they replied. "He is God, the One, our Lord! How can we stop what the Lord wills to be so?"

The Dawn Star listened to their questions and concerns and formulated a plan.

"Listen to me, my host."

All eyes were upon him.

"Heaven is our home. The city of God belongs to us. It is our desire …" He paused to choose another word " …our will that heaven be for the angels alone and no one else, am I right?"

"Yes!" came the collective agreement from the host.

The Dawn Star continued, "If that is true, shouldn't our collective wills be greater than the will of one being? What of our desire and wishes? What about what we want? Do we want our songs silenced by the songs of humans?"

"No!"

"Do we want them sharing heaven with us?"

"No!"

"Are we going to let the One force us into loving them?"

"No!"

"Will we let the will of the One supersede our will?"

"No!"

"Can we trust God anymore?"

With that question, there was no immediate reply from his host. A timid voice spoke up from the now silent group and said, "But He's the Lord, our Lord … isn't He?"

"Is He?" The question snapped sharply from the Dawn Star's lips. "Is He really our Lord when He decides to give them everything, even that which belongs to us? It is clear to me that the One is putting the needs and desires of the woman and the man ahead of what we want. Is that fair?"

Murmurs of no filtered through the crowd.

"We were here first!" the Dawn Star continued. "As far as I am concerned, when the creatures of the dust became more important to the One than us, He stopped being *our* Lord. We can no longer trust Him to do what's right for heaven … for us!"

"If we can't trust in God, who can we trust?" someone spoke out.

The Dawn Star smiled and knew the time was right.

"Me," he said. "You can trust me." He paused to take in the effect his words had upon his host. "I know what you need and want … what we all need and want," he continued as he swept his arms across the room.

"As difficult as it is to comprehend, it's clear that the One has let us down by taking heaven away from us and giving it to them."

Even more cracks appeared on the walls and ceiling, unnoticed.

"We can't let that happen … I won't let that happen!" he shouted.

A loud agreement rose from the crowd to punctuate his words.

"You can put your trust in me! I'm Lucifer, the Dawn Star! I am the Light Bringer! We bring light upon what God wants to do with our home for all of heaven to see. It will not be the city of man! It is and always will be the city of angels! Let the creatures of the dust have the Earth … let God keep His precious creatures down there where they belong." The last of his words came out as a loud, venomous hiss, followed by an equally loud, angry agreement from his angels.

"Heaven is ours!" he shouted.

"Yes!" came the response.

"Heaven is ours!" he repeated even louder.

"Yes!" they responded in kind.

"Heaven is ours!" the Dawn Star shouted again.

The host began to repeat that phrase over and over until it became like a chant.

"And I will lead you!" he shouted over the crowd.

Another loud "yes" rose from the crowd in unison.

Soon another phrase began to mingle with the others until they were the only words that could be heard. The Dawn Star paused to listen. When he understood what was being said, he smiled, closed his eyes, raised his head, and stretched his arms wide as if to receive fully what they were saying.

"Lord Dawn Star! Lord Dawn Star! Lord Dawn Star!" The words were repeated over and over.

He rose to the very apex of the ceiling. When he opened his eyes, he looked down and observed his entire host on their knees as they continued to chant and pay homage to him.

The Dawn Star was overwhelmed with a feeling he had never experienced before. He knew the joy of singing and the thrill of excitement as he watched the world being formed. But never before had he experienced the euphoria of being worshipped, for that was indeed what was happening with his host. He was being worshipped. The more they worshipped him, the more he wanted of it. He took it all in until the sound of the cracks appearing on the walls became loud enough to drown out the noise of the angels.

Suddenly, the tabernacle shattered in a great crystalline crash. Shards rained down upon those inside … Then the Dawn Star and his host were gone, along with the tabernacle of praise.

REBELLION

When it is written of the rebellion in heaven between Lucifer and his angels against God and the heavenly host, much will be said of it and great power will be given to it. In truth, it was over practically the same moment it was decided upon.

After the tabernacle of praise crashed to the ground, the Dawn Star and his host found themselves poised over creation, facing the cathedral windows of God's holy temple. It appeared to the Dawn Star that the rest of the entire host of heaven was gathered there. It had never occurred to him before this moment how vast that number was. They were gathered in ranks and layers in front of the temple, stretching out wide and upward.

The first rank was made up of the host of Michael, with the archangel in the center. His host stretched to the left and right of him, curving around in an arc as if to surround the Dawn Star and his host but not quite. Only the boundaries of the city of God were being blocked.

The Dawn Star noticed each of Michael's host held a sword with both hands at their chest, elbows extended outward, with the blade pointing straight up in front of their faces. The Dawn Star couldn't help but be a little struck by the precision of Michael's host. At the same time, he was taken aback by this display of force, if that's what it was.

In the next several rows and layers above Michael was the host of Gabriel. They were not ordered in as precise a fashion as Michael's ranks, but they managed to create an impressive and powerful impression in any case.

As he observed the ranks, the Dawn Star noticed Gabriel positioned near the top in the center with Gloria and Allegro standing directly to the right and left of him respectively. He looked at them, and surprise registered on his face. A part of him felt betrayed to see them standing there with Gabriel. He did not necessarily feel betrayed by Gloria and Allegro but rather by his brother archangel, who he felt might have taken two of his most gifted host from him … for himself.

As the Dawn Star continued to survey what was before him, he saw the One at the very peak of this gathering. His features were lost in the glory surrounding Him. The One was completely engulfed in a light so bright that the Dawn Star could not look directly upon Him. He dipped his head and shaded his face with his hand in a vain attempt to diminish the power of God's glory presented before him.

As he attempted to hide himself from the glory of God, the Dawn Star became aware of something strange and unfamiliar that made him feel intensely uncomfortable. For the first time in his life, he was afraid … of the One.

As his mind raced with thoughts of what was happening, a singular voice broke through the noise in his head. It was Gloria's, and she was singing.

"Holy, holy, holy is the Lord of hosts! All heaven and creation is filled with His Glory!"

The Dawn Star was familiar with this tune, for he and Gloria had sung it together many times at the tree of songs and in the tabernacle of praise, which now lay in ruins on the other side of the city of God.

As she repeated the chorus, another voice joined hers in harmony. It belonged to Allegro. They sang it together several times. Eventually they were joined by the voices of all the host of heaven gathered in and around the holy temple.

As they sang, the glory of the One grew brighter, if that was even possible. It was so intense that the Dawn Star and his host had no choice but to turn their backs to God and His temple.

The song continued for quite some time, repeating over and over. Under different circumstances, it would have been the Dawn Star leading this choir of heaven. Now instead of joining in the joy of the moment, he could only listen as if he were forced to do so and was tortured by the sound. Somewhere deep inside him, his heart broke because he could not bring himself to sing along with them. None of his host who hovered above creation with him joined their voices to the chorus. They were truly set apart from the rest of heaven.

When the song finally came to a conclusion and all of heaven was still and quiet, the Dawn Star heard the familiar voice of the One speaking to him as if He were directly behind him. He turned around to see the One was still at the temple, seated high and lifted up, His glory diminished but not to the point that the Lord's features could be distinguished as before.

"Why are you here?" asked the One.

"You know why," answered the Dawn Star.

The One remained silent. After a moment, the Dawn Star

continued, but he spoke loud enough so the entire host would be able to hear him.

"We don't want them here, the beloved. Heaven is our home. It belongs to us!"

There was no reply from the temple. He continued, but this time he addressed the entire host of heaven.

"Do you know what the One is planning for the beloved? Eventually He plans to bring them here, to be with Him, with us. He will give everything we have to them!" he said, letting his anger punctuate the last word. "We can't let that happen!"

The Dawn Star turned around to indicate his host. As he moved closer to the temple, he said in a loud, menacing tone, "We won't let that happen!"

Immediately, Michael's voice penetrated the moment with a booming command. "At the ready!"

In an instant, his host moved as one, leaning toward the Dawn Star and his host with their swords poised toward him.

The Dawn Star took note of the swooshing sound the multitude of swords made in unison as they quickly came into a new position. It reminded him of when he and the One had entered the room of readiness and he had made the same sound with one of the swords hanging there. Was this moment the purpose, the reason for the room of readiness?

"Brother, you must listen to me," he said to Michael.

"Come no farther!" Michael said.

"I … we only wish to talk with the One, to reason with him, with you all. You must allow us to approach the temple," he said as he moved closer to where they were gathered.

"No!"

Instantly, Michael's host encroached upon the Dawn Star.

He looked around at Michael and his host and said in a gentle, pleading tone, "Brother, why are you doing this? I just want to talk to the Lord. Why won't you allow me to pass?"

"It is for your protection," the voice of the One answered, sounding as if He was right next to him, though He could still be seen at the temple, some distance away from the Dawn Star.

"Protection from what?" the Dawn Star asked, clearly confused.

"Your present condition."

"What condition?"

"An unholy condition," said the One in a gentle, matter-of-fact manner. "That which is unholy cannot approach that which is holy. Your decision to incite rebellion among your host and go against what I have willed to be so from the beginning has made you unholy. If you were to cross back over the boundaries of heaven as you are now, it would destroy you."

This revelation from the One took the Dawn Star by surprise and shocked his spirit down to its very core. It was the fact that God had declared him to be unholy and unfit for heaven that was the most devastating to him, not the decisions and choices that had brought about the change in his condition.

How can this be? he asked himself. He was an archangel in the kingdom of heaven. He was the first, created from the glory of God. He commanded a great host. He was the Dawn Star who sang all the songs of creation. His was the first star in the morning. If anyone was deserving of heaven, it was him. But now God was declaring the Dawn Star unworthy.

"How can I be in the condition you say I am in?" asked the Dawn Star. "I am still an archangel. I don't feel unholy. I only want what's best for heaven, for all of us. What's so wrong with that? I still love You and serve You."

"But do you, and will you, love all that I love?" asked the One.

The Dawn Star answered quickly, "Yes! Of course! I would and do love all that you love!"

"Even the beloved?" the One asked gently.

It was then that the Dawn Star felt the now familiar darkness grip his heart tighter at the mention of the beloved.

"Why is that so necessary?" the Dawn Star asked with an edge to his voice.

"Because love is at the very heart of who I am. When you love Me, you love what I love, all that I love, especially the beloved. Love is at the center of the kingdom of heaven."

The Dawn Star knew this to be true, for he had experienced the fullness of what the One was describing firsthand. He had been aware of it at the beginning of his life, through the creation of all things. Even at the western sea when he confronted Him about the song the man sang in the garden. He slowly came to the realization that he had separated himself from experiencing the love of the One when he sang the doors of the tabernacle closed for the last time.

The One continued, "You and your host now stand separated from all that heaven truly is. Was that your intention?"

"Of course not!" declared the Dawn Star. "Heaven is our home! We want it to remain our home." He put an emphasis on *our* to drive home his point. With that, the Dawn Star broke off the conversation with the One to address the host at large.

"I want you to know why we are here!" he said loud enough for all to hear.

"Then tell them," said the One, whose voice now came from the height of the temple instead of directly by the Dawn Star.

All eyes of heaven now focused upon the Dawn Star and his host suspended above creation.

"The kingdom of heaven is our home!" he declared loudly and triumphantly.

His host around him gave a loud agreement to his statement. "Yes!"

"It is the city of God!"

"Yes!" his host cried.

"It is the city of angels!" the Dawn Star continued, slowly building in volume and intensity, while his host continued to urge him on in loud enthusiastic affirmation. "Yes!"

As the Dawn Star spoke, he began to slowly rise above his host as he had in the tabernacle of praise. "We were all made from the glory of God! We were all made for heaven! Heaven is ours!"

At the climax of his words, his host responded with an even louder, elongated affirmation for what the Dawn Star was declaring. It continued for some time until the Dawn Star, who was still positioned above his host, slowly bowed his head as the crowd grew quiet.

The Dawn Star then spoke in a grave tone, allowing a hardness into his voice as he rose to the same level as the One at the top of the holy temple but still some distance from him.

"But the One, the Lord God almighty has just declared that we …" He paused and swept his arms to indicate all his host. "… that we are not fit for heaven anymore!"

There was a corporate shout from his host.

"Do you know why?" he said and then paused for emphasis. "Because we don't agree with the plans God has for heaven! That is why we are here, fighting for *our* home!"

"Our home!" shouted his host.

"We don't want to share heaven, our home, with the humans, the beloved! He is going to give everything to them! That was God's plan all along!"

From the Dawn Star's elevated position directly across from the One, he slowly turned to face all the host of heaven.

"We can't let that happen! I won't let that happen!"

As he ended the statement, he looked defiantly at the One. It was then that the Dawn Star heard the One speak to him in such a way that He could have been right next to him. All other noises seemed to disappear for him.

"Stop this now," the voice said gently. "Turn away from this plan and return to Me."

"You know I can't and won't," said the Dawn Star.

"All because of the beloved?"

"Yes!"

"Why?" asked the One.

"You know why," said the Dawn Star with an edge.

"Tell me," the voice implored softly.

"Because You gave them … You will give them everything!" the Dawn Star said, shouting it in his head.

"Yes, that's true. But this isn't about everything, is it? This isn't about heaven or about My love for them. This is about the one thing I have given them that is a part of Me that I have not given to you … isn't it?"

"Yes!" he shouted.

Though the conversation was spoken silently between the them, all of heaven heard the angry affirmation from the Dawn Star. He composed himself and continued to speak silently to the Lord.

"They are not worthy of this gift. They are not worthy of anything You are going to give them, much less the gift of creativity. They are not worthy!"

"But you are?"

The Dawn Star knew this was what he was feeling but was hesitant to admit it.

"You want this gift for yourself only and no one else, not even your brothers, don't you?"

Again, the Dawn Star had to admit the truth, but he said nothing. Ever since the song in the garden, he could think of nothing else. The desire for the gift of creation possessed him above all else. This thing, to the Dawn Star, diminished all the other attributes he had been given, even his voice and his songs, which were the shining jewels of who he was. His very identity faded into the shadows in the light of that which he coveted. The Dawn Star changed his tone.

"Don't You see? If You were to let me have this gift, it would mean we could be even closer than we were because I would have a part of You, Your love, that no one else had." He paused and had a thought that grew into another desire in his mind and seemed to eclipse all other desires in his heart. "It would be like we were one together."

The Lord was silent.

After a moment, the Dawn Star grew impatient and said, "Give it to me."

It was less a request than a demand. At any other time in his life, he would never have thought to speak to God in such a manner. Perhaps it was the separation from heaven or the present condition the Lord said he was in that put him at distance from the holiness of God.

"You do not know what you are asking," said the One. "I ask again, Lucifer. Stop this now and return to me."

To the Dawn Star, even though the One was still at some distance from him at the holy temple, it felt as if He were pleading with him from His very soul. For a moment he wanted to acquiesce to Him. He felt as if a choice were being put to him: return to the Lord and be content with all that he had been given or embrace fully the covetous demands of his own heart. For quite a while, the Dawn Star hovered above his host in silence, feeling the full tension of his choices alone.

Then from his host below him, he became slowly aware of sounds and words that had now become familiar to him. His entire company was chanting slowly and methodically in increasing volume what had been heard in the tabernacle before it was destroyed.

"Hail Lord Dawn Star! Hail Lord Lucifer! Hail Lord Dawn Star! Hail Lord Lucifer!"

As the chant grew louder, the same sense of euphoria he had felt for the first time in the glass tabernacle came washing over him. All thoughts and tension of the choice put before him was gone. There was only this moment with his host and the intoxication of their adoration.

Is this how the One felt to be worshipped? To be at the very center of any given moment? Now this moment was the Dawn Star's. As they chanted, the Dawn Star closed his eyes, drew back his head, and spread his arms wide to try to take in every bit of what was being offered to him. At this moment, nothing else mattered, not the One, not his brothers, not heaven, and certainly not the humans. This was all that mattered to him right now. This was his time, the time of the Dawn Star.

The moment was cut short when a shout came from the temple, drowning out the chants of his host. It was the booming voice of Michael.

"Who is the King of glory?" he shouted.

"The Lord strong and mighty is the King of glory!" came the loud reply of the heavenly host gathered at the temple.

Michael shouted louder, and Gabriel joined him. "Who is the King of glory?"

"The Lord strong and mighty is the King of glory!" came the response.

By this time, the chanting of the Dawn Star's host had silenced completely. All that could be heard was the declaration and response of the angels of heaven.

This was repeated over and over, and then another sound joined in. It was the sound of Gloria and Allegro singing a doxology. They were joined by half of the heavenly host present with them.

"Praise God from whom all blessings flow. Praise Him all creation and heavenly host. Praise the One, the Father, the Spirit, and Son."

The song and the declaration became as one hymn, providing a perfect counterpoint to each other.

As he listened to all this, the Dawn Star couldn't help but notice it was the most beautiful sound he had ever heard come from heaven. He was silent as the praise to the One washed over him and took away every bit of euphoria he had felt from the adoration of his host. He slowly came to realize that it would always be temporary and would never last, but praise to God would be something that could, and would, go on forever.

During the praise, the Dawn Star and his host became aware that the glory of God from the temple was slowly becoming larger and getting brighter. They felt compelled to join their voices to the song, but they found they couldn't. Their voices were gone. They couldn't sing.

They were surrounded by the glory of God and the sounds of worship, but they were helpless to be part of it. It was all taken from them. They looked to the Dawn Star helplessly, pleading for something to be done. Grief and fear was etched upon each of the host. Faces that once reflected all that was beautiful, joyous, and good were now twisted and changed by the same fear and grief.

As the Dawn Star looked upon his host, all he saw in their eyes was the anguish of betrayal. They did not count on this. Then a bolt of fear raced through him. He tried to open his mouth to sing, but what came out was a tuneless, scratchy noise. He made several more attempts with the same result. He realized his voice was gone. The time he had sung the doors of the tabernacle of praise closed was the last time he would ever sing again. No one would ever hear the songs of the Dawn Star again.

With that, the Dawn Star screamed in anguish, followed by the laments of his own host.

By this time, the glory of God had reached its zenith, and the echo of praise was now fading. The only sound heard was the mourning of the Dawn Star and his host over the loss of their voices.

The Dawn Star looked around at them. They who were once, in his eyes, the brightest stars in heaven were now crumpled in on themselves as if they were deflated and a light was extinguished from them. They looked like dark blemishes against the pure, holy background of God's glory around them. Nothing else could be seen. Instead of feeling sympathy and sorrow for them, the Dawn Star was disgusted by them. Something he had never felt before.

He still hovered above them, surrounded by the glory of God, when he shouted in an angry scream, "Why have you done this? You have taken everything from me!"

In answer, the plural voice of the One penetrated through the moment in a loud, authoritative tone almost completely devoid of warmth.

"Lucifer! You who were the Dawn Star, the singer of all songs, are found in judgement of a covetous and selfish heart. You have incited rebellion in the midst of my host … You have refused to accept My will for all of creation. You have become an enemy of all that is holy and good. You are an enemy to the heavenly realms and to the Lord

God your Creator. You are no longer the Dawn Star. You are the adversary … You are Satan!"

With that, the glory of God withdrew from around them, revealing creation below his feet … and then he who was the Dawn Star … fell.

THE FALL

The first sensation Lucifer felt when he began to fall was fear, accompanied by an overwhelming sense of helplessness. As he watched the golden vistas of heaven shrink in the distance, his limbs flayed about in the void, trying to reach for something, anything to stay his decent, but to no avail. His wings, gifted to him by the One, which enabled him to travel wherever he wished, were now useless to him. He could not will them to do his bidding as before. As he fell, he observed bits of his wings fly up from him and beyond. As the last vestige of heaven disappeared from view, he began to fall through the dark vastness of space. It was then that he began to feel something never before experienced by anyone: pain.

It started gradually but built in intensity as he fell. The blackness of space disappeared as Lucifer was completely engulfed in light, but not the light he was accustomed to. It was the light of the flames by which he was now surrounded. As the pain increased, so did the terror of what was happening to him. It felt as if every aspect of who he was, was being torn and burned away from him.

As the Dawn Star, he had been the singer of all songs, but the only song for the agony he was experiencing came out as a wordless scream. No vestige of his once incomparable singing voice remained. If it could be heard in the vacuum of space, it would be comparable to the worst sound of terror one could imagine from any living thing.

Lucifer burned and screamed past swirling galaxies and nebulae. He burned and screamed past seas of asteroids. He burned through the atmosphere of Earth and crashed down upon a rocky promontory on a tall, steep mountain, the creation of which he had witnessed firsthand. Finally, the burning ceased as his journey came to an end.

In the garden, some distance away from where Lucifer lay exhausted, the man and woman took a moment to marvel at the bright object streaking across the daytime sky, pointing at it and exclaiming over this new wonder. Then they went about their tasks for the rest of the day.

Lucifer had no recollection of how long he lay on that stone cliff when he finally opened his eyes to discover his new reality. At first, he remembered very little of the fall except for the intense pain that had seemed to last for an eternity. His body felt heavy as he attempted to raise himself up to sit, which took a great deal of effort.

When he sat upright, he took time to observe his surroundings. He saw that he was atop a high mountain surrounded by other mountain ranges almost as equally high. He could see patches of green vegetation tucked in the valleys far below. The place where Lucifer sat was bleak and colorless except for green in the distance and the brilliant blue sky above him.

Before his fall, Lucifer would have found great beauty in his present surroundings, as they were part of God's perfect creation. Now it was different somehow. To him in his present circumstances, it felt lifeless.

Which brought to him another new sensation that he had never experienced before. He was alone. He had known fear, and he had just experienced physical pain, but in his entire existence he had never known what it was like to be truly alone. Even when it was just him and the One, it had been more than enough. Now that he was away from all that was familiar to him, he was realizing that being apart from the One was truly agonizing. It tormented his spirit far worse than the flames from his fall. As he sat and watched the sun make its way through the sky several times, he understood that his loneliness may be a permanent condition.

For several days, perhaps even months and years, he sat and brooded on that gray desolate peak over thoughts and questions for which the answers would not be forthcoming. The most prominent question that echoed in his mind in silence was why. In his mind, he replayed the events that had transpired at the temple of heaven just before the fall and could not come up with any reason that made sense to him for why he fell, why he found himself expelled from heaven.

He recalled the words of the One when He accused him of inciting rebellion. To Lucifer rebellion had not been their intent. Their intent was to preserve and protect what had belonged to them from the very beginning … To Lucifer and his followers, they were seeking only what was fair and just for themselves.

Had he fallen because the One had declared him unholy and therefore unfit for heaven? Even now he could not bring himself to believe it. He was of heaven. Nothing he could think of could change that fact in his mind. Lucifer decided that nothing God said about him before he fell was true. He was who he was and would be forevermore an archangel of the heavenly host, the Dawn Star, and singer of all songs!

That thought seemed to rally his broken spirit and created in him a resolve to somehow return to heaven and prove to God that the Lord was wrong about him. He struggled to get to his feet. It felt as if there were a great weight around him, pulling him back down to the ground. After several laborious attempts, he was successful in standing upright in spite of the heaviness he felt all about him.

In heaven, there had been no sense of weight, only lightness in every sense of the word. He had been able to move effortlessly and without hindrance. Even when he had visited Earth countless times, he had felt nothing like what he was feeling now. Had his fall changed him somehow? Was he now cursed to be burdened with this weight, whatever it was, from this moment on?

As Lucifer stood there, he was also aware of constant pain in every part of him. It was nowhere near the intensity of what it had been during his fall, but he felt it nonetheless. He took a step forward, which made him cry out. After several steps, he realized the pain was something he would have to deal with. He would struggle through it, though he'd never had to struggle through anything before in his life.

Eventually he made it to the edge of the promontory and looked down at the valley below. He found himself drawn to the lush, rich, varied tones of green stretched out before him. He recalled the first time the color was seen upon creation, the day God had spoken the trees into existence.

With that memory fresh in his mind, Lucifer reached out with his hand as if to touch them. It was then that he noticed his hand for the first time. Gone was the bright, glowing golden hue of his skin. In its place was a charred, reddish semblance of what was once his hand. He cried out in shock and looked at his other hand. It, too, was changed. With that sudden movement, he lost his balance and fell off the ledge and experienced falling for the second time in his life.

Lucifer tumbled down the steep slope of the mountain for what seemed like a long time. He finally came to rest among a grove of trees surrounded by rocks and boulders. The ground was covered in a wide variety of plant life.

He had experienced some pain as he descended but not to the extent of the flames from the first fall. He attempted to sit up and lean against the tree that was evidently responsible for stopping the momentum of his fall. He sat for a moment to clear his jumbled mind and to get his bearings. It seemed as if he were completely surrounded by green except for the stark gray boulders.

Though he had experienced the Earth and its innate beauty many times as an archangel, it felt different in his present circumstances. The various tones of green and the details of leaves in each plant stood out to him. It was as if he were experiencing them for the first time. He reached out a finger to the leaf of a plant next to him and caught sight of his charred reddish fingers. He nearly cried out in despair but heard a sound coming from a short distance away.

He found it difficult to stand because of the trauma caused by his most recent fall. Instead, he crawled through the vegetation toward the sound, which ended up belonging to a small brook that was making its way through the wood.

He found the sound soothing to his troubled spirit, and it gave him renewed strength that allowed him to stand. Carefully and slowly, he followed the course of the stream through the wood until it opened into a small clearing, revealing a crystal pool at its center.

He made his way to the edge of the pond, where the water, undisturbed by the stream flowing into it, created a perfect reflection of everything surrounding its banks, including Lucifer.

At the first glimpse of the reflection looking back at him, he cried out in surprise. Lucifer had no understanding of the stranger staring back at him in equal surprise.

He recalled that the first time he had seen his own reflection was in the eyes of the One when he was first brought into existence. It was a bright golden creature of light that he remembered, not the charred, dark ruined figure he saw staring back at him. He cried out in a loud voice, fell to his knees, and struck his new image reflected in the water. It disappeared in the disturbance of the surface, only to reappear when the water settled again.

He struck the surface again, screaming all the while like a wild, crazed animal. The water splashed up on him, but he felt none of its coolness upon his skin. He felt nothing but anger and rage as the image returned to mock him when the pond settled back into its stillness. There was nothing he could do to change who he now was.

He was no longer the Dawn Star. He was a shadow of that image, nothing more. He was the singer of all songs, the most beautiful voice in the universe. The One had declared this to him on the edge of the western ocean. At that thought, Lucifer closed his eyes and strained to remember at least one of the songs he had learned from the tree of songs, but to no avail. He could only muster snippets at best from his memory. He was not able to bring forth even a semblance of a tune with his singing voice, which was now gone. It was clear that everything he had was stripped from him, burned away by the fire as he fell.

As he stared into the water at his ruined visage, Lucifer longed for just a glimpse of what he used to be. He gazed at the water until the sun went down and the darkness of the night closed around him.

He found the darkness strangely comforting. In the light of day, he was faced with the reality of what he had lost. It seemed to scream the truth of who he now was with every beam of light that showed through the branches. It was a reminder of the heavenly light that had been taken from him. In the shadows of the night, when the sun went down, the true nature of objects were hidden, their details blurred into a mirage of their true nature, including himself. He was hidden in the sweet, comforting cloak of darkness. He could gaze into inky blackness and see whatever his imagination, fueled by his memory, desired something to be.

When he looked up through the branches of the tree he was leaning against, he could imagine he was beneath his beloved tree of songs and the stars winking through the silhouetted limbs could easily be the light fruit growing upon it. At some point, he could look to the eastern horizon and see his star shining there. Then the dawn came, spreading the truth of his reality with the slow, deliberate rising of the sun and causing his star to disappear in the pink light.

The dawn was silent. There was no one to sing in the morning, for that was Lucifer's task and his alone. It was just as well he couldn't sing it; he wouldn't sing it, even if he had a voice for the task. When the day fully arrived, the feeling of despair brought on by the truth of his new reality washed over him in waves.

Each day, Lucifer returned to his vigil at the pond's edge, for he thought if he concentrated enough, he could will himself into his former image. He would close his eyes and imagine what he was like in heaven, his hair of gold, his opalescent skin that shimmered in the light, his bright golden eyes … and the wings of an archangel.

In his former life, Lucifer found he was the master of his own will. Whatever he had desired to do or wherever he had desired to be, it was all accomplished with the speed of a thought. But his wishes and desires in heaven had been somewhat limited in that he had only wanted to be with his brothers, his host, or wherever the One desired him to be.

Now, earthbound as he was, his will was held captive by the limitations of this world … by a heaviness he could not explain. In the presence of the One, there were no limits within the boundaries of His will. There was an ease, a lightness, in heaven that came seemingly without effort. Here in creation, on his own, it seemed that everything was difficult for him, especially alone as he was.

Why was that, he wondered. Lucifer had not been alone in his rebellion. His host had been with him in every aspect of the confrontation before the holy temple. Where were they? Why was he alone in his exile? Surely they were as culpable as he?

The more he thought of them, the more he realized that his heart was changing toward them. Where he had once held them in great regard and esteem, he now held them contemptible as he remembered how they pathetically cowered before the glory and force of God. He wondered why it was easy to turn them to his will with a few choice words and a slight manipulation of the truth. In retrospect, it seemed far too easy to influence them to his will.

One day, when he opened his eyes while sitting at the pond's edge, he caught a glimpse in the water's reflection of an image of his former self. He immediately held up his hand, only to see the gold of his skin fade back to his present reality. He was not sure if what he saw in the water was the truth or merely an illusion created by a memory. In any case, whether it was a mirage or truth didn't seem to matter to Lucifer. He wanted to see it again.

Buoyed in his spirit, he concentrated again, striving to create what he saw in his mind reflected back at him in the water. The effort was so intense that he felt pain throughout his body, but he paid it no mind as a golden figure slowly materialized in the reflection on the pond. He looked at his hands and saw they were indeed changed. He felt the gentle weight of wings between his shoulders … Then he screamed out in agony as he collapsed to the ground. The pain faded as the illusion of his former self faded away. Evidently trying to return to his original formal glory came at a price, and the price was pain.

He lay by the pond's edge for several cycles of the sun before he made another attempt and another after that and then another … always resulting in intense pain and a collapse to the ground. Was this to be his life on Earth? A life filled with pain and disappointment? Was he ever to be free from it? Was this what the humans in the garden experienced? Intense pain and disappointment over trying to achieve one's desires and failing, or was it just relegated to him alone? If that were so and he was alone in his agony, he found it unfair and unjust that he should be made the only one to suffer.

Gradually, after several days and weeks of trying to look like himself again, he discovered he was able to hold the image longer each time before the pain became unbearable. It seemed that pain was his constant companion. Even in his current form, the heaviness he had felt constantly since being earthbound always pulled at him in the form of a dull ache, which he experienced in every part of his being.

The only exception was during the night when he seemed to get a respite from the weight of life. During the daylight hours, he could never escape from the truth of who he was. Each glimpse of himself in the reflective waters of the pond or glance at his hand was a painful reminder of who he was now. But at night, when the sun was gone and the shadows took over the landscape, it was as if he disappeared into dark inkiness. Without the constant reminder of the truth, the pain would subside somewhat, and he became lighter. Was that the answer? To disappear? All through the night, Lucifer pondered that idea. Would the troubles of this new life go away if he could just disappear?

That next morning, Lucifer made his way to the edge of the pond and peered at his scarred and ruined reflection. He began to will the visage before him away. To his surprise, it took very little effort on his part and very little time for his image to fade from view. He looked at the rest of his body as little by little he seemed to simply disappear. His surroundings hadn't changed. He just wasn't there anymore. But more to the point, the heaviness that had been his constant fellow since the fall was gone as well, replaced by a lightness that was almost like the lightness of heaven. The deep pain he constantly felt was reduced to a dull ache. He decided he could live with that.

In this incorporeal form, Lucifer found he was not bound to the natural laws of the Earth. He could move easier and faster. When a small breeze made its way into the clearing where he stood, he discovered he could move with it like he was part of the very air itself.

The breeze made its way up the mountain slope, carrying the adversary with it to the ledge where he had first fallen. By this time, the dull ache he felt grew stronger until it surpassed what he experienced on a regular basis. When the pain was at its worst, he willed himself back to his former appearance. The intense pain was gone, but the heaviness had returned.

He pondered why his existence was so difficult among creation, with the constant pain, heaviness, and frustration. Why was it so hard for him? Perhaps it was because he was not created for this place. He was created for the city of God, from the glory of God. He was not of creation. He was of heaven. He was made to be with God. The One must have known what would happen to him down here, what it would be like to be separated from all that was familiar to him. If God really knew and understood the agony of being separated from Him, away from His presence, *He wouldn't have sent me here*, he thought to himself.

As he sat and brooded these questions, the sweet cloak of night embraced the peak with its shadows. He welcomed the darkness, which seemed to match his thoughts and eased his troubles. Whatever comfort he could experience in his present condition, it came with the night. He could hide in the dark. But even in the shadows, he could not escape the inevitable truth that he was alone. For him perhaps the loneliness was the greater form of punishment. Was it always to be this way? For here there was no one like him. What would become of him without the fellowship of his brothers, his host, and the One?

He gradually realized that he was not alone on the Earth. Somewhere there was a garden where the man and the woman lived. Lucifer seemed to have forgotten his deep resentment of the humans and only longed to be where they were. Perhaps in a way, it would ease his constant loneliness.

"Why?" he asked himself. Was the loneliness so unbearable to him that he was willing to seek out the company of those he considered to be his adversary, his Satan? Was it because he knew the beloved were the focus and object of the One's love and to somehow be near them was to return to the presence of God?

A new purpose began to consume the adversary. He must get to the garden. He must get to the beloved. The way to Eden was unclear, but the method of travel was not. He would make himself one with the air and travel upon the winds and currents that constantly moved across the Earth. When the cloak of night lifted the next morning, Lucifer disappeared into the atmosphere of creation in search of Eden.

He discovered it did not take long for him to find. He wasn't exactly sure how he fell upon his course of action, but for someone intimately familiar with the presence of God, he let that be his guide and indication as to where the garden of Eden could be found. It would be surrounded and engulfed by His love, which was almost as visibly present as He was. As he got closer to his goal, he became aware of it. It was like he was discovering something from the point of view of an outside spectator rather than a participant. Eden appeared in a valley as the wind he was with traveled up and over a set of hills. By this time, the pain brought on by keeping himself invisible for so long got the best of him.

He dropped to the ground, having returned to his corporeal form, such as it was, just behind a small stand of rocks. He would hide himself there until the night came with its blessed shadows.

He did not know what accounted for his desire to stay hidden in the shadows. Perhaps to Lucifer to be seen was to be known as he was now. He knew deep in his heart that in this state he could not allow himself to be fully known. If he appeared at all, it would be in the form of an illusion of what he once was or how he wanted to be known.

As the Dawn Star, he was an archangel filled with the glory, strength, and power of heaven itself. This was what he would hold to be true even though it wasn't and never would be again.

When night came, he left the shelter of his rocks and began to move up and through this small valley. He climbed up to a rise in the landscape only to have his breath taken away by the sight that lay before him, for down the hill and a cross a patch of brush and stones lay the boundaries of Eden.

Lucifer had seen and visited Eden on many occasions, but this was the first time he had seen it at night and from an earthbound vantage point. He could not deny its beauty, which was rivaled only by heaven itself.

Instead of being engulfed entirely by the shadows of night, the garden took on a light of its own as plants and flowers displayed a luminescence that bathed the landscape in a variety of pastel colors. While he had observed some animals that were active during the daylight hours settle to rest when the evening came, he discovered there were creatures that became active in the night. Colorful insects filled the night air and darted about like stars that had flown down from the sky. Maybe he had seen hints of this in the great library in the palace of all things, but they had failed to grab his full attention. With every fiber of his being, he found himself longing to be there. If this was the closest he would ever be to heaven again, then that was his desire.

He did not see the man and the woman from his vantage point. He surmised that they were within the interior of the garden, away from hedges and foliage that surrounded it and served as an indication of its boundaries.

The night faded as the sun rose, and the garden was restored to its emerald glory of the day. As his protective shadows disappeared, Lucifer willed himself to be invisible with the air. The temporary respite from the pain and heaviness was a welcome sensation and served to buoy his spirit and resolve to enter the garden. In this form, he would be able to enter unseen and detected. But as he approached the boundary, he was unable to enter. It was as if he were being stopped by a wall as invisible as he was.

He tried several times to gain entrance but with little effect. The breezes that blew across the land were able to pass through, for he could see the wind's effect on the trees on the other side of the boundary. Birds and insects could fly in and across freely, unencumbered.

For the rest of the sun's journey across the sky, Lucifer looked for a way in. He circumnavigated the entire exterior of the garden, searching to gain entrance, but to no avail. He also sought away over the invisible wall, but he was also denied. The entire garden seemed to be enclosed by a protective barrier. It reminded him of the crystal dome of the cathedral of praise, which now lay in ruins in the city of God.

By the end of the day, he fell, exhausted and in pain, and hid himself in the shelter of the rocks. But more than anything, he was done in by the frustration of his failure and the realization that perhaps the invisible boundary was there specifically to keep him, Lucifer, out.

All through the night, he brooded on that thought and the injustice of it. How could the Lord to this to him? He felt an anger burning against the One, something that up to this point he had somehow kept in check but that now had fully sparked into ignition. Perhaps before he had hung onto a small hope that he might someday return and be restored to his former glory in heaven. But now he felt his anger burn away that hopeless dream to ash, along with any desire to be by the One's side again.

All his life, Lucifer had known and experienced the love of God firsthand. In his present mindset, he began to question the truth of that love.

"If the very heart of God is love, how could it be love when He is so willing to banish one of His beloved archangels just because I don't share His passion for the humans? If He could do this to me so easily, what would He do to His 'beloved' when they fail Him? Which they will. I have no doubt. Then we will know the truth of God's love. He called me His adversary. Then His adversary I will be," he declared to himself.

Just before dawn, as the violet of night began to fade, he looked to the eastern horizon to see his star, as he was in the habit of doing since his exile. But instead of his star, a black dot had appeared in its place and was growing in size, like a hole in the sky. In the distance, he heard a sound as if a thousand voices were screaming at once. Then he saw a group of lights clustered together streaking toward the hole. As the lights grew nearer, the sound of what could only be described as terror grew louder and more deafening. As they moved through the sky, the Dawn Star saw them change from a bright light to a dark gray color, like a sooty smudge against the sky, until they, as well as the sound, were swallowed up by the hole. In the next instant, the hole shrank and disappeared, and then there was silence as the day made itself known.

Lucifer sat in the deep shadows of his outcropping of rocks to ponder what had just happened. The streaking lights and screaming burned and echoed in his mind. As he thought, he couldn't shake the feeling that something about what he had just experienced was very familiar.

His thoughts were interrupted by another sound, one far more pleasant than the last one, coming from the direction of the garden. He disappeared and made his way toward it. When he arrived at Eden's hedge boundary unseen, he looked over into the garden itself and observed the woman picking some fruit from one of the trees and gathering them into a grass basket. She was singing. It was a song he had never heard before.

Despite himself, Lucifer found the song strangely moving and sweet in nature. Her voice seemed to flow from her like the lilt of a brook. He closed his eyes to listen, a slight smile crossing his face. He opened his eyes when he heard another sound join the woman's voice. He looked and discovered that the man was sitting beneath the shade of the tree from which the woman was gathering fruit.

He was holding something to his mouth, a stick, and blowing through it and working his fingers across its length to create a sound of music Lucifer had never heard before. Up to this point, the only music Lucifer had heard was that which came from his own voice or the voices of the heavenly host. But now music was being made through something else.

He could not deny the beauty of the simple, haunting sound from the man's instrument. It seemed to mingle perfectly with the woman's singing. At some point it took on a countermelody, creating perfect harmony. The lilt of their joyful laughter at the end of the song provided the perfect conclusion to the piece.

He stood there invisible and mesmerized by what he was hearing. The wonder of the music created in him a profound sense of awe similar to what he had experienced when he witnessed the One speak creation into being. There was no doubt that there was a piece of that in what the man and the woman had created together.

All day he observed and listened until the sun began to set and he could no longer maintain his invisibility. He returned to the shelter of his rocks, strangely moved by what he had just experienced. Even in his present condition, Lucifer had an innate sense of awe and wonder for what was created, even that which came from the humans.

As the night settled in, he listened to the songs coming from the garden and the voices of the man and woman. Theirs were the only songs he had heard since his exile. He no longer heard the songs of the Earth and heavens. Until he'd heard the song in the garden, the world had been silent to him, which only seemed to add to the anguish of his life, feeding into his anger, frustration, and jealousy. In his mind, Lucifer had taught all creation to sing, and now he was unable to hear what had first come from his mouth. He could hear the sounds of nature, but he could not hear the music he had taught them. The music coming from the garden was beautiful but foreign to him, leaving him feeling like more of an outsider and a stranger.

He was brooding on these thoughts like open wound that he was allowing to fester when a familiar voice from behind broke in and interrupted the process.

"It is beautiful, isn't it?"

Lucifer turned around to see the One standing there in His glory. The last time he had seen the Lord, His features were hidden by an abundance of light and glory. Now, even though the light was being manifested around Him, he could see the face of God smiling at him as if He were greeting an old friend.

"You're here!" he said with surprise.

"I have always been here. I am with Eve and Adam in the garden, I am in the kingdom of heaven, I am wherever I desire and need to be. I have been with you."

This declaration confused and frustrated Lucifer to the point that his next question came out edged with anger.

"Why haven't I seen You or heard from You all this time?"

"You haven't been looking for Me, have you?"

"I didn't know I could …" Lucifer said as much to himself as to the One.

The Lord smiled and asked, "Did you like their music?"

Despite his feelings toward the humans, he responded in the only way he truthfully could.

"Yes, I did. It was beautiful." Lucifer was then still and quiet for a few moments before he asked, "Why are you with me now?"

"To bring you home."

As the One said it, He looked directly into Lucifer's eyes, but to Lucifer it felt like God was looking directly into his soul. His heart leaped with joy at the thought of returning to heaven.

"Why? Why now?" Lucifer asked.

"Because you don't belong here, and I think you've come to that realization yourself."

He couldn't deny that wasn't true. Everything was difficult in creation, at least for someone like him. The pain and heaviness of this life were constant reminders of what he had lost in the fall. He found almost everything he did or desired to do he had to learn. Heaven wasn't like that. Everything came easily to him compared to this. Was it difficult for him because he wasn't of the Earth, or was it a permanent condition of life apart from the kingdom of God? He was about to let the One know he was ready to come home. Then a question came to his mind.

"If You knew it would be so difficult for me, why did You send me here?"

"There was nowhere else for you to go. Your choices brought you here."

Lucifer wasn't aware of any choices that would warrant a fall from heaven, at least none that he would admit freely to himself. Another question came to his mind.

"Why am I here … alone? What happened to my host?" Whatever wrong the Lord had declared him guilty of, Lucifer knew he had not been alone in committing his infractions. "Are they still with you?"

"They were sent away by their choice. I gave them the opportunity to stay with Me and in time I would have restored them back into My kingdom. They didn't want to be there without you. Most all of them made that choice. A few chose to remain."

"Where did they go?" As he asked the question, he knew the answer, as he recalled the screams and the streak of light in the early dawn being swallowed up by the hole in the sky. "That was them, wasn't it?" In thinking about it, he recognized the voices of his host in the midst of the terror.

The One simply nodded.

"Where were they sent?" Lucifer asked.

"To the place that is the farthest from where I am."

"What is it?"

"It will come to be known as the abyss."

"And the few who chose to remain with you? What of them?"

"It is for Me to know alone," the One answered.

After a moment, Lucifer's face screwed into a confused expression. "Why wasn't I sent there? To the abyss."

The One was quiet for a time until He said, "Because you were the Dawn Star, and you never bowed down to anyone but Me."

Lucifer was taken aback by the Lord's statement, surprised that even in the state he was in, he felt like he was being commended for something, forgetting for a moment that he had been the object of his host's worship.

The One continued, "It was My desire to restore them back into My presence if that was their choice. That is always My desire."

"What about me? Can I be restored?" Lucifer asked.

"That is why I am here, to offer you that choice. Do you want to come home?"

Lucifer was quiet. Hearing that question brought a lightness to his heart that hadn't been there since the fall. He wanted to shout out loud, "Yes! With all my heart!" But he remained silent as another song from garden made its way to the rocks where he and the One stood. It was Adam's voice singing another song Lucifer had never heard before.

He looked at the One, who stood taking in the song and listening intently, a smile playing across His face. When the song came to completion, Lucifer asked another question.

"This morning, the man had a stick that made music."

"Yes, he did," the Lord replied.

"Did you give it to him?"

"Not directly. He made it himself from the materials in the garden and learned to make music from it."

"He created it," Lucifer said with a deep sigh.

"Yes, he did, and it's beautiful," the One looked to the garden with the expression He'd had after every day of creation when He declared what he had just made was good.

"If I made the choice to come home," Lucifer said, "it wouldn't be the same for me, would it?"

"No. It wouldn't," the One replied. "It would be different. Something new."

"My host wouldn't be there."

"No."

"I would be alone then. I wouldn't have anything or anyone that's mine. My voice is gone, the tabernacle is gone, my host is gone."

"You would still have Me; I have always been with you. I want to redeem you and create a new purpose for you. You will start over and live in My house forever."

"But so will they," he said, nodding his head toward Eden.

"Yes. They will always have me, should they so choose. My plan has always been to have them with Me in creation as well as in heaven. It is My deepest and greatest desire for them."

The words of the One stung his spirit. The idea of heaven for the humans was what had inspired his rebellion in the first place. An idea began to formulate in his mind that might allow the circumstances to turn in his favor.

"I would like to come home," he said. "Give me what You gave to them and I'll come home. If You love me as You say You do and want to give me a new life, give me that. Let me create. Give me what they have, and I will be glad to share heaven with them."

The One was silent as the songs from the garden continued. Then he said, quietly pleading, "Just come home."

"Why?" Lucifer asked, raising his voice.

"You don't belong here."

Lucifer exploded with anger, pointing to the garden. "And they don't belong in heaven!" he shouted. "If they were created in Your image with that ability, won't they think that they can be Your equal?

Won't they try to take heaven from You and make it their own?" The lies first articulated by Lucifer in the tabernacle seemed to now flow from his mouth with the same ease as before.

The One stood quietly and listened. Then He simply responded by saying, "All that I have is theirs, as they choose to remain with Me."

In another outburst, Lucifer shouted, "*They are not worthy!*"

The night grew quiet, and the silence seemed to engulf them both.

"Come home. Let Me be enough for you in heaven," the One said.

For an instant, Lucifer felt the urge to acquiesce and give in to the Lord's plea. Then another thought, a realization, filled his mind, giving chase to that instant urge.

"You don't want me with You," Lucifer said. "You don't want me down here with them."

God said nothing.

Lucifer felt a surge of satisfaction as if he had unlocked a hidden mystery, a secret truth. He laughed and said, "That's it, isn't it? You think I'll make trouble for them." Feeling somewhat victorious for the first time since his fall, Lucifer sat down on a stone. He felt justified somehow.

The One stood still and quiet, looking at Lucifer. His glory grew brighter and surrounded Lucifer. The adversary looked up as visions of the city of God, his brothers, his host, the holy temple, the Lord speaking creation into life filled his sight. He was shown a vision of himself singing in the dawn of each day. He saw himself and the One standing before the tree of songs for the first time and Gloria and Allegro singing with him as they sat in the branches of his beloved tree.

The visions amid God's glory continued as a picture of Lucifer as the Dawn Star sang with the man and the woman a song that had come from them came into his view. In the vision, he was smiling and laughing with them.

Suddenly he stood, waved the glory away, and firmly said, “No!”

All was still and quiet for a long while. The warm colors of a new day began to peek above the horizon. Lucifer observed his light, the dawn star, sink from view as he felt the last visages of his old life fade away with the memories of the vision in God’s glory.

The One walked to him and asked, “Is this your choice?”

Lucifer did not see the love and compassion in the One’s face as He asked the question.

“Yes!” Lucifer replied. “Up there”—he looked up into sky—“You called me Your adversary. Then so be it. Your adversary I will be. I will prove to You that they are not worthy of anything You have given them or will give them, including Your love. As You loved me yet still rejected me, discarded me … so will You reject and discard them.”

The One said, “It won’t be easy. They will have more power than you think. They can and will, with my help, resist you … Even when it seems that you are winning the hearts of men and women, you will fail … You have failed. I will be with them. Even when they do not choose to be with me, I will continue to love them fiercely and passionately. You will not win.”

With that, the One was gone as the light of morning filled the sky, turning it to bright blue.

It was several days and weeks after the One left him on Earth that the adversary, after several attempts, found a way into the garden, even if it was by accident.

For many days, in his invisible form, he had observed creatures, especially the smaller ones, come in and out of the garden effortlessly. *Perhaps*, he thought, *if I made myself like one of them, I could slip through the limbs and branches of the protective hedge unnoticed.*

Perhaps this way he could bypass the invisible barrier that thwarted his efforts at every turn.

His memory took him to the images in the room of God's word and a picture of a small, green, slender creature that would one day be called a snake or a serpent. He decided this was the form he would take.

Keeping the image in his mind, he concentrated with great intensity. But just as before, willing himself into another form took a great deal of time and effort. Finally, he was successful. He'd been standing unseen by the boundary, but in his new form, he suddenly found himself falling to the ground in great pain, where he thrashed about in agony. He was not sure if he cried out. If he had, it would have been barely audible. Perhaps that was the reason he found himself in the slender hands of the woman, who had reached over the hedge to rescue him.

In a pleasant voice filled with kindness, she asked, "Oh, little one. How did you get out here? Come in here with us."

As he was being lifted up and over the hedge, he heard the voice of the man ask pleasantly, "What is that you have there?"

The woman lifted her hands to show him. "I found this little thing on the other side all alone."

The man smiled at the wriggling form that Lucifer had taken. "Well, that won't do. Bring it in here with us."

Just then, the pain was so intense and he thrashed about in so much agony that he fell to the ground and returned to his invisible state. Surprised by the creature's sudden disappearance, the man and woman laughed. Then they strolled back into the interior of Eden as if nothing had happened.

So, all I needed to get into the garden ... thought Lucifer, *was an invitation.*

After recovering from the ordeal of his transformation, the adversary followed the man and the woman farther into the interior of the garden in search of a dark, shady place he knew of, to a certain tree that reminded him of a tree he had once known in heaven. There he would hide in its shadows … and wait.

EPILOGUE

Gabriel walked slowly through the gates to the city of God, having completed his mission. This now was the way to enter heaven from creation.

Since the fall, they no longer used the three open cathedral windows to descend to the Earth, for the creation was not open to them anymore. Any access to it and its inhabitants came by the One's command alone. The only view observed from God's holy temple was of the swirling golden clouds that had been present before creation, before the waters. Now the full knowledge of what went on beneath that golden vista was privy to only the One.

Gabriel's memories of the Dawn Star's fall and the aftermath were vivid in his mind. He recalled his brother Michael, upon the Lord's request, retrieving the flaming blue sword from the palace of all things and going with it to Eden to guard the way to the tree of life.

Gloria had been sent by the One to the tree of songs to obtain one last unsung song from its branches. As she had carried the large light fruit out of the chamber, the amethyst doors had closed and had remained unopened since. Gloria had brought the orb to God's holy temple, where it waited until the time came for its song to be revealed.

Everything had changed just as the One said it would if the man and the woman ate from the tree of the knowledge of good and evil, which they did. They had made a choice that changed destiny for all of creation, and death became the enemy of life. That day, everything born, everything that had come into life, began to die. The songs of creation were never heard again.

Perhaps it was due to Lucifer's influence that Adam and Eve fell. Perhaps it was a choice made completely of their own will and desire. Or perhaps it was both. But the result would have been the same: a life filled with wonder and joy would now be accompanied by hardship, sorrow, and death.

Gabriel would never forget the day Adam took his last breath on Earth. For some reason the One had asked Gabriel to accompany Him when the time grew near. Perhaps He didn't want him to die alone. He was very old by then. His beloved Eve had died many years before, and the grief and pain of that loss had weighed heavy upon his narrow shoulders for the remainder of his weary life.

He was in his makeshift garden, singing the song he had first sung in another garden a long time ago and far away:

> My Father is the Lord of all creation,
> and I give Him all my love.
> This garden is His, which He gave to us,
> the water, the earth, and the sky above.
> Thank you, Father. Thank you, Father …

At the last note, Gabriel watched as the One knelt, placed his mouth on Adam, and took away the breath He had first placed within him the day the man had become a living soul. It exited his body in the form of a barely audible "whaaaaaa." After the kiss from God, the lifeless form of the first man collapsed into the dust.

The One stooped down, gathered him into His arms, and cradled him. They then traveled a short distance to a stand of rocks where the body of Eve lay. The rocks were removed, and God bade Gabriel to gather her up and place her in His arms along with her husband.

They returned to heaven, with the man and the woman being carried by the Lord. Gabriel noticed the lifeless forms in the arms of the One now resembled what they had been when they were first taken from the Earth in the beginning. The ravages of their life and death on Earth were erased from their faces. They looked as if they could wake from their sleep and return to their life in Eden.

The One left Gabriel at the jade doors of the palace of all things and continued on with man and the woman alone. Gabriel surmised that there was a place in the green fields of heaven where the Lord would lay them together, where they would always be remembered and loved.

Looking at the Lord with the two of them in His arms, Gabriel realized that in the One was the great capacity to love and in the midst of that love was the enormous ability to forgive. After all that had happened, He still loved them and wanted them with Him. Was there any love and forgiveness left for Lucifer, who was so bent on destroying everything in creation that God had called good? That knowledge belonged to the One alone.

The adversary's influence had infected the whole Earth. There was not one person who had not been touched by the stain of sin. Even those who God deemed to be those after His own heart were affected by it. It was that stain that kept them from the One. But that would change.

Gabriel pulled himself from his memories and began to climb the golden staircase leading to God's holy temple. He saw the One waiting for him at the top.

"It's done," he said. "She knows. The girl, Mary, knows what will happen to her."

“Thank you,” the One said simply.

Gabriel stood for a long time by the One until he spoke what was on his heart.

“Lord … she seems so young,”

The Lord just smiled to Himself and said, “She will be wonderful.”

Sometime later, heaven was going about its business in all corners of the city of God, when a sound never before heard in heaven filled the air. It was a steady, rapid, soft, rhythmic, swishing sound that went on continuously. All stopped whatever they were doing.

The One smiled, closed his eyes, and listened to the sound with the greatest intent. It was the sound of hope and a new beginning. It was the sound of joy for all in creation trapped by the inevitability of death and the influence of the adversary.

All in heaven stayed still and quiet and listened to the fetal heartbeat of the Son of God.

… And so it began.

Printed in the United States
by Baker & Taylor Publisher Services

Printed in the United States
by Baker & Taylor Publisher Services